EARTH MAGIC

Physically and mentally scarred after a terrible accident, Claire is bullied by a gang of youths one day while walking through the park — and then Jake steps in to help. Working with him in his garden, Claire finds peace and a purpose in life, along with the first steps towards friendship and, perhaps, even love. But the harsh practicalities of their lives threaten to terminate the enchanted hours they spend together on the allotment, and Claire begins to wonder if she and Jake can ever have a future together . . .

LINDA M. PRIESTLEY

◆

EARTH MAGIC

Complete and Unabridged

LINFORD
Leicester

First published in Great Britain in 2012

First Linford Edition
published 2014

A catalogue record for this book is available
from the British Library.

ISBN 978–1–4448–2190–1

Published by
F. A. Thorpe (Publishing)
Anstey, Leicestershire

Set by Words & Graphics Ltd.
Anstey, Leicestershire
Printed and bound in Great Britain by
T. J. International Ltd., Padstow, Cornwall

This book is printed on acid-free paper

For my Mother Veronica and
my Mother-in-law Hilda
who both enjoy a love story

And for Dave, Jo and Alex,
as always.

1

Claire sat on a bench in Victoria Park and watched people go by: kids on trikes and bikes, breath misting around them as they laughed, wrapped up warm against the brittle cold; parents smiling, enjoying their antics; excited yells; dogs bounding after sticks; kids kicking balls around. It was a hurdy-gurdy of sounds and sights revolving round her, barely touching her in her little bubble of isolation. She huddled further into her coat to make herself invisible, and licked the ice cream bought on impulse from a van doing a surprising amount of trade considering this was a chilly Saturday in February.

In the distance, across the park, a young man was running along the perimeter path: lithe, pace easy as a cheetah's, beautiful to watch. He seemed to be doing a circuit of the park, and if so, should be passing Claire shortly. He vanished behind some shrubbery and it was as if the sun had gone behind a cloud.

Three lads and a girl walked past, smoking something they shouldn't, judging by a faint sickly smell wafting towards Claire. One lad stopped and stared frankly at her. 'Get a look at that!' he yelled. His friends stopped, turned, and stared.

Claire put a hand to her face and felt the shiny skin and crumpled ridges. Damn, damn, damn. She pulled the pashmina up over her head, hiding most of the damage — that pattern of scars which marred her face. She'd forgotten to put on her camouflage makeup that morning because she'd been so upset and desperate to get out of the flat. Damn; that explained the funny looks from the kid in the ice cream queue.

'What a crocodillopig,' the second lad said. 'If I looked like that I'd wear a paper bag over my head.'

'If I looked like that, I'd top meself,' squealed the third, a runty-looking kid, and they all laughed.

Claire pretended she hadn't heard and looked away, but that made it worse, because the horrible yobs hovered on the periphery of her vision like evil sprites. She stood up and walked away casually, heading in the direction the yobs had come from. She heard footsteps behind her and glanced back. They'd turned and were following her.

'I think she's a lizard escaped from the zoo,' said the girl.

'Or her mum humped a snake.'

'I wouldn't give her one if you paid me.'

'Maybe if it was dark, I would.'

Claire shoved her hands in her pockets, nails digging into the palms. Her jaws clamped together and she could hear her rapid breathing sough over her teeth. She picked up her pace. So did they. She recalled news items

about people being beaten up, mur-
dered even, just because of the way they
dressed or the way they looked. But the
park was full of people; they wouldn't
attack her in broad daylight just
because of her scarring. Would they?

'You lot are disgusting. That's really
spiteful.' A new voice, rich as drinking
chocolate. Claire swung round to see
the runner she'd admired earlier grab
the third boy's spliff, chuck it to the
ground and grind it into dust with his
heel. 'You shouldn't be smoking that
and you know it. You lot should be
ashamed, being so cruel. Now shove
off, and if I ever hear any of you
speaking to anyone like that again I'll
see you get nicked for it. And that
includes you,' he said, pointing at the
third boy.

The biggest lad went up to the
runner, chest to chest. 'So what?' he
sneered, blowing dodgy smoke in the
runner's face. The runner stood there
impassively, staring the boy down.

The third boy grabbed the first boy's

arm. 'Leave it. C'mon . . . Please . . . '
The yobs moved off and turned with
vulgar hand signals before wandering
away.

Claire found herself staring up into
the runner's deep brown eyes and stam-
mering her thanks, unspent adrenaline
running through her veins like static.
She clamped her jaws down on the swirls
of dizziness engulfing her.

'You OK?' said the runner.

She heaved in a deep breath. 'I am
now, thanks, but wasn't that a little
risky?'

'No . . . '

She swayed. He caught her with
strong hands. 'Let's sit down a minute,'
he said. 'Do you want to go to the café
for a coffee or something? You look
really upset.'

Claire was far too shy to say yes, but
her mouth couldn't say no, not with her
heart still thudding away inside it.

The café was just a short distance
away. 'You're shaking. I insist.' He
groped in his tracksuit pocket, and then

smiled in a relieved way. 'I've got some cash; come on. My name's Jake.'

'I'm Claire.' It would be rather nice to sit down with this hot guy and let him cosset her with a cappuccino, so she could pretend that she was normal and they were going out as lovers. She'd always been a daydreamer, though dreams like this filled her with melancholy nowadays. Even so, in her dreams she could be unscarred, whole, and dreams were better than nothing. 'Thanks,' She let him lead her to a seat, which he tucked under her solicitously as she sat. It was aluminium and shockingly cold. She gasped from it, and they both laughed and relaxed.

'You sit there and I'll fetch,' said Jake, an easy grin spreading over his face. 'What'll you have?'

As he fetched her coffee she studied his back. Even snuggled in a tracksuit, she could see he was well-proportioned, broad shoulders narrowing to his hips. The way he stood suggested pent-up power. She felt her hammering pulse subside back to normal, only to rise again as Jake turned round carrying a tray. He handed her a coffee topped with froth and sat opposite, with a mug of hot chocolate with cream. He gave that heart-stopping smile again.

'Thanks.' Claire picked up the spoon and scooped a mouthful of chocolate-sprinkled bubbles into her mouth. 'I'm sorry. I've distracted you from your run. Are you training for something?'

There was a slight hesitation before he said, 'No. Just getting fit. Do you run at all?'

Claire snorted a giggle out. 'Not likely. I wouldn't know where to start.'

'I haven't seen you here before. I often run round the park. I'm sure I'd have noticed you.'

Noticed her? Noticed the girl with the horrible scars on her face? 'I come quite often, especially during the week. But I walk rather than run. Gets me out of the flat.'

'I tend to come early, when nobody else is around. The park is magical

7

then, especially if there's been a frost.'

'Maybe that's why then. I come later in the day.'

He was staring frankly into her face. Normally she hated that, really hated people staring. They could look, they could even ask, but she hated them staring, especially on the sly. Sometimes they seemed to think she wouldn't notice the stares, the second glances out of corners of eyes. Sometimes there would be a clash of eyes and the starer would look away, abashed. Claire would smile to make it all right, but it never did make it all right, not really.

But the way Jake was staring at her was very different. He was looking into her eyes for one thing. Just as Claire was thinking this, his gaze dropped to the cappuccino. 'I just love the way you do that,' he said in his velvet voice.

'What?'

'Spoon the froth into your mouth.'

'I love cappuccino coffee. I love the bubbles. And there's always a rim of bubbles left when the coffee's drunk;

I'm not wasting that either.'

He smiled and took a big swig of his chocolate. Claire burst out laughing.

'What?'

'You've got a blob of cream on your nose. Here . . . ' She took a serviette and wiped it off him. He grinned that gorgeous smile again. His head would dip slightly, then the smile would slowly develop as he looked at her bashfully with his deep brown eyes.

'Thanks for your intervention earlier,' she said. 'I was getting really scared, you know. I . . . I normally wear camouflage paint over the scars and they don't show up, but today I just had to get out of the flat and I forgot.' There — she'd mentioned the scars. In case he hadn't noticed (as if).

'No probs. You've got your own flat, then?'

'Ha, I wish. No. I live with my mum. I just got another job rejection. It upset me, and it upsets Mum to see me upset, if you see what I mean, so I came out for a walk, that's all.' Aware she was beginning to gabble, Claire fell silent and thought back to when her mum handed her the thin envelope. Thin was bad, because it would contain no contract to sign. Same as usual: 'Dear Ms Smith, thank you for your application for the post of Legal Secretary with Radley & Babcock Solicitors. We regret to inform you that your application was unsuccessful on this occasion. We would like to wish you all the best for the future.' Blah blah. She could write them herself. Claire poked at the coffee. 'I spent a year away from home doing a Legal Secretary course and it's got me nowhere except into debt.'

'I know what you mean. I've got three A-grade A-levels, and a B, but I can't find full-time work, and it's been two years now. Sometimes I don't even get a reply. But I . . . ' he broke off and shrugged.

'Bad jobs market,' said Claire, trying to sound grown-up about it. 'Employers want experience, and that's hard to get.'

'Vicious circle,' he agreed.

Claire felt oddly comforted by this exchange. She'd assumed the reason she'd been rejected so many times was that she literally didn't present a very good face in interviews. But maybe it was just the economic climate after all. She smiled, looked at Jake, then bit a lip. 'Are you cold?' He was wearing a tracksuit but not much else. She was swathed in her thick winter coat, and the chilly wind was nibbling her ears.

'A bit,' he confessed. 'I'm dressed for running, not sitting.'

Bother. Now he'll go and that'll be the end of it. She wanted to ask for his phone number, ask where he lived, but it would be too pushy. She knew he was just being a gentleman talking to her like this; that he couldn't possibly be interested in her as a woman, despite being fascinated by the way she drank her coffee. She drained her cup and spooned the rest of the froth into her mouth.

'I'm tempted to buy you another, just to watch you do that all over again.'

'It's my round next. I think we should go Dutch anyway if you're out of work too,' she said. 'And anyhow, I can't let you freeze on my account. Have you far to go to get home?'

It was a deliberate question, of course. *Please let him live nearby. He seems such a nice bloke — a real gentleman. Mature too.* Even if he was unlikely as a boyfriend, Claire badly wanted him as a friend. Her other friends had drifted away after the accident, when she dropped out of the circle of friends and into hospital. They'd been great at first, visiting her, keeping her up-to-date by posting on her wall on Facebook and so on, though the 'likes' and comments on her wall had dwindled until she'd stopped posting because she hated the thought that she was talking to herself. She'd had to take a year out from school, and when she went back she was in the year below and didn't mix so much. It was as if people were scared of upsetting her, so they avoided her. Her old friends left school, some to university, others into jobs. Facebook was the only contact she had with them now, and even that was sporadic. She looked at their pages but hardly posted anything. College had been OK; she'd made a few friends, but that ended, and everyone went their separate ways.

'Earth to Claire . . . Earth to Claire . . . you're miles away. I just said I live on the Arrandel Estate.'

Claire dragged her mind back to the present with a start. 'Oh sorry, yes; miles away.' Uhoh. The Arrandel Estate was quite the worst place in town, or so her mum said when they were house-hunting. It had a bad reputation and was often in the news for lawless goings-on. Better to buy a flat in a good area than have a house with a garden on that estate. Claire would have laid money on those yobs living there. 'That's handy for the park,' she said, a shade too brightly, pulling herself back from another reverie. 'I live on the other side of the park. Fountain Court, Rendlesham Drive. The flats. It's handy for the park too.'

'Nice flats there. Quite posh. I run along Rendlesham Drive sometimes in the evening when the park's locked up.'

'I wish we had a garden, though. I miss the garden we had when we lived in a house. I really like gardening and it's really frustrating when all I have is the balcony. I used to have a tiny veg patch when we lived in a house, just like Dad. I miss it.' *I miss him.*

'Let's go for a wander round the park,' Jake suggested, standing and coming to move her chair for her as she stood.

She flashed a smile at him. 'Nobody's done that for me for ages. Grandad always used to help Granny into her chair and Dad would stand behind Mum and tuck her chair in, then help me. That was before Dad died, of course. Mum and I are much more slobby now; TV dinners and all.'

'Your dad's dead? Sorry to hear that.'

'Yes, and my gran and grandad, on both sides.'

'Oh. Sorry.' Jake looked away.

Claire half hoped he would take her hand in his . . . just for comfort, say; nothing more . . . but he didn't, though they matched each other's pace, at ease in each other's company. It was nearly lunchtime and the sun was about as high as it was going to get. The frost had gone and it was one of those days where the parts of you in the sunshine get warm while the rest of you is cold.

'Oh no,' groaned Jake. In the distance but coming towards them were the yobs, still mucking about, running heedlessly over the flowerbeds. 'I can't face them again. Come with me. I've got something to show you.' He led her to a gate in the perimeter fence and she followed him unthinkingly, heedless of any danger. It wasn't until they were walking down a narrow footpath hemmed in with the park boundary on one side and a thick hedge on the other that she remembered that she'd only known Jake for an hour or so. He could have been leading her anywhere.

2

'Where does this lead?' she asked suspiciously.

'A surprise.'

It was hardly reassuring as an answer once her common sense had kicked in, but she followed him nevertheless. A few minutes later they found themselves in some overgrown allotments: cold frames made from old windows, rusting corrugated iron, weeds, even some scrubby trees. There were some well-tended plots fighting against the dereliction at the far end of the site and, nearby, a couple of cultivated patches like islands in a sea of grass.

'Wow. I never knew these were here,' said Claire, rushing on ahead with delight. 'Why are so many of them covered in grass?' Jake didn't answer, but perhaps he hadn't heard as she'd rushed along the path without him.

An old man was hoeing some weeds on one of the island patches nearby. He scowled at her, squinting against the sun. 'This is private property, allotment holders only.' He turned away and carried on hoeing.

'Sorry.' Claire stopped abruptly, put her hand to her cheek, pulled the Pashmina back over her face, turned to see where Jake was and almost bumped into his chest.

The old man looked up again and smiled. 'Ah, it's OK if you're with Jake. About time you came and tended your plot, young man. I thought mebbe you'd given up.'

'I've been busy,' said Jake defensively. 'And I've been to pick my sprouts and stuff. I just haven't done much else. It is winter after all. I've been trying to get fit. Running.'

'You can get fit digging,' grumbled the old man. He was wearing an old cloth cap and a coat which looked as if it might have seen service in World War II, but he seemed sprightly enough. His

18

hoe sliced through a rash of weeds which had had the temerity to grow during the winter. 'You want to get your winter digging done so the frost can break it up. Lazy scamp.'

Claire looked at Jake, six feet tall, sweatshirt draped off his cliff-like chest muscles, and thought the epithet rather ridiculous.

'Claire, this is Ted. Ted, this is Claire, a new friend.'

Ted stopped hoeing, wiped his hand on his trousers, which Claire didn't think would help much since they looked grubby too, and offered her his hand.

She shook it. 'I never knew there were allotments here. If I'd known . . . ' If she had known, she would have rented one ages ago when they'd first moved to the flat, and grown all the things she wanted to instead of cramming a few plants onto the balcony. Maybe she could have brought plants and cuttings from the old house, plants which she remembered her dad tending. A poignant stab hit her between the eyes, making them water briefly.

Most of the site was a wasteland of grass, but Ted's allotment was well-tended with leeks and sprouts, curly kale, and lines of other vegetables that Claire didn't recognise because her dad had never grown them. She gazed curiously over the plot, thinking, remembering. She touched her face.

'How's your family? How's that rapscallion Toby?' Ted asked Jake.

'Mum's fine, thanks, Ted. Toby? Huh. I'm well annoyed with him and I don't even want to think about him just now. I came to show Claire my allotment. Not that it's much to look at this time of year.' Jake led her over tufty grass to an allotment as isolated as Ted's. It had a ramshackle shed on it with a small, crazy-paving patio, a garden bench, some mature fruit trees pointing naked fingers to the sky, and a patch of herbs. There were Brussels sprouts, and a bed which had obviously had leeks in until recently, with outside leaves carelessly dropped on the surface. There was also a long row of over-wintering broad beans.

The weeds were beginning to take over. Jake surveyed it all with a dismayed look on his face. 'I have rather neglected it,' he conceded ruefully.

'I'd love to have an allotment,' said Claire. 'Are they expensive?'

'Yes, they are now. £50 a year. Ripoff. Mum says she thinks the council are trying to put people off having them so they can sell the land.'

'Oh shi . . . sugar. I can't really afford that.' Claire looked round at the sea of grass. 'And it looks pretty daunting. I can't even see where the other allotments are.'

'If you were serious then I'd suggest taking one between mine and Ted's and using weed-killer to begin with. But look, mine's a bit too much for me to look after, especially . . . why don't you share mine? At least at first.'

'Really? You really mean that? And you wouldn't mind if I did my own thing on it, like grew flowers as well as veg?'

'Grow what you like. Or just give me a hand whenever you want. Whatever.' He shrugged those powerful-looking shoulders.

'Oh Jake, thank you.' Claire flung herself at him and hugged him before her brain caught up with her body. The scent of warm masculinity flooded her with strange emotions. 'Oh, sorry.' She stepped back and blushed.

'Oh, don't be sorry.' He gave one of his heart-stopping smiles.

Just then Claire's tummy let out the most enormous gurgle. She put a horrified hand to her mouth, and they both burst out laughing. 'How unlady-like,' she apologised. 'I'd better go home. Mum's making soup and she's expecting me. Would you like to come for lunch?'

Jake thought for about a minute, then screwed his face up. 'Best not. I'd love to but I ought to go home. My mum'll be back from the surgery and, well, you know . . . '

'Surgery?'

'She's a receptionist at the doctor's surgery in Erranby, and Saturday emergency surgeries are always bad. They get patients from other practices on Saturdays.' Erranby was a town about ten miles away. He pondered for a few heartbeats. 'Look, do you fancy meeting me back here this afternoon? Ted's right. I've neglected this. My grandad would freak.'

'Your grandad?'

'This used to be his. Then when he was ill I'd give him a hand. I did more and more while he did less and less, sitting in an old chair by the shed telling me what to do, until he had to go into hospital. Then . . . afterwards, well, I kept it going in his memory.' Jake shrugged helplessly. 'When we were small we'd all come over — Mum, Granny, Grandad, Toby, me. It was great. Toby loved it too.' A look of yearning and regret passed over his face.

'I'll be back,' Claire promised. 'Two-ish? And can I have your phone number just in case?' They swapped mobile numbers and she walked home with a huge smile on her face.

★ ★ ★

'Hello love,' said her mum, Elizabeth, as Claire walked through the door. 'Nice walk? I was just beginning to worry.'

'Oh Mum, you always worry.'

'I'm a mother; it's in the job description . . . Oh sorry love, careless words . . . Soup?'

'Please. I'm starved.'

Over lunch Claire told her mum a little about Ted and about Jake, but not where he lived or one or two other trivial details. She said he was just a friend and that she was going to help him on his allotment.

Elizabeth gave a big smile. 'Really?

Oh that'll be good, love. Get a bit of fresh air in your lungs.' The smile slipped a little and her mum looked away. They drifted into silence as they finished their lunch and washed up.

After lunch Claire retreated to her bedroom and sat at her dressing table. As always nowadays, she forced her thoughts into neutral as she reached for the pot of camouflage paint. Thinking was dangerous. Thinking allowed the demons into her mind like viruses. One glance was enough to show her that Jake would only ever be a friend. Nobody could fall in love with that face. She applied the makeup swiftly with practiced ease until her reflection, whilst not attractive, was at least superficially acceptable to other people. Her lustrous hair was dark and long, and her eyes sparkled like sapphires — her best features, her dad had said before the accident. After the accident he never mentioned her looks at all, not once to the day he died. Even before the fire she'd never thought of herself as beautiful, and now she tried not to think of herself at all.

When Claire was about to leave for the allotments, Elizabeth scrutinised her with an amused and knowing quirk on her lips. 'Don't you think you're a little overdressed if you're mucking around on a muddy allotment? Go on; I know you have some tatty old jeans and you are not going to wear your new coat if you're doing some digging, surely?'

'But Mum . . .'

She was right, of course. Claire stomped back into her bedroom and changed her best clothes for something older, but not as scruffy as the jeans Elizabeth suggested.

Jake's face lit up. 'I was worried you might not come back,' he said. 'I've brought the shed key. It's full of Grandad's old tools. You can use some of those if you like.' He unlocked the shed.

Claire peered inside, flinching at a spiderweb by the door, brushing it away with her hand. 'Yuck,' she said, shuddering, 'I hate it when you walk into webs all unexpected and they cling.' She peered round. An old spade and fork hung on a wall, with shears, loppers and secateurs in a basket on the shelf. There was a can of oil, a couple of old kitchen chairs and table, and some sort of stove with a tatty old kettle on it, as well as a hoe bandaged round the middle and a rake made with four-inch nails. Claire lifted the fork. It was heavy, with a polished handle and tines worn from years of use. She trod it into the soil under a clump of grass on an untaken allotment, and heaved. There was a snapping of roots. She pressed harder, feeling the strain in the handle before the clump lifted and turned over. Yellow wiry roots infested the clump and would take ages to pick out. 'Oh crikey. I don't think I'll take on a new allotment, not just yet. I'm glad you're sharing yours with me.'

'Me too — glad, I mean. That's couch grass and it's a flipping menace.

Let's get started.'

Claire noticed for the second time that Jake minded his language. It wasn't what she was used to, where the 'F' word was used by herself and all her old friends like some sort of punctuation. Her mum wasn't too keen on the word, and Claire only used it in her mum's presence when they were having 'words' (which never helped). She realised she'd better watch it round Jake as well.

'You tell me what needs doing.'

Jake asked her to dig over the old leek bed to tidy it up, putting the rubbish on the compost heap while he tackled the older weeds. The soil was claggy and cold but soon she was hot. They conversed in gasped-out snatches of conversation. Come half-three she was tired out and her hands were filthy and cold. She hadn't had so much fun in ages. Jake cast a speculative eye inside the shed. 'We could bring some tea and coffee down here. I never bothered on my own, but now . . . '

Seemed like a plan.

Claire took the grubby kettle home, though. If she was going to have coffee made with water boiled in it, she wanted to make sure it was clean and free of spiders.

3

Next day, Sunday, Claire bounced out of bed early. She normally lingered quite late, especially at the weekend, because there wasn't much to get up for. During the week she'd do a few chores while her mum was at work, maybe look for jobs online, maybe read for a while. She took a mug of tea into her mum's bedroom. 'I'm off to the allotment.'

'Don't overdo it,' said Elizabeth, groaning into the pillow.

* * *

Jake wasn't there when Claire arrived, so she phoned him. 'I'm about to have a shower after my run,' he said. 'I was going to church with Mum but as you're there I'll skive this week. I'll see if I have a spare key for the shed to let you have and I'll be over soon.'

While she was waiting, Claire had a snoop over the allotment site. The main access was along a narrow track next to an old, closed junior school, too narrow for a vehicle, but wide enough for a wheelbarrow. It looked as if manure and compost had to be barrowed in by hand, then. Maybe this was why the allotments nearest the school entrance were nearly all taken, with Jake's and Ted's like islands of cultivation in the sea of grass and weeds in the hinterland. Nobody was working on any of the allotments and they had a desolate look of winter neglect about them, though they were cultivated, save for a couple which were covered in grass. She turned and started back along the footpath towards Jake's allotment. There was a figure in the distance. He waved. Jake. Her heart somersaulted and she told it to behave. Jake was just a friend. He was a gentleman, and that was why he was so polite about her face. She touched her face, reassured that she'd remembered the camouflage makeup today. *Don't get any foolish romantic ideas,* she told herself firmly. *You start swooning over him and he'll run a mile, and you'll be a billy-no-mates again.*

As she reached Jake's allotment she handed him the kettle, now at least clean if not actually gleaming — the soot had defeated her even though the kitchen sink now bore some very strange black marks all over it.

'I'll show you where the standpipe is,' he said. 'We're not supposed to attach hosepipes but I know the School-Enders do to theirs.'

'School-Enders?'

'Yeah, those who have allotments near the old school.' He lit the stove and unpacked some mugs and tea bags, and a packet of biscuits. 'We'll need to keep them in a tin in case of mice.'

'Thanks for that; too much information,' said Claire with a grimace. 'What are we doing today?'

'Winter digging. The soil's heavy clay

32

and this helps break it up. That's what Ted says anyway.'

It took Claire a little while to get into the rhythm of it. Although she'd had a small patch of garden at her last home, she'd never deep-dug such heavy soil. The routine soothed her as if grooming her jumbled thoughts. The smell of rich broken earth drifted up to her nose. She inhaled deeply. 'Looks nice as chocolate.'

Jake threw a smile at her. 'You wouldn't want to eat it though.' He started digging again. Claire watched the graceful rhythm of his muscles as he turned the soil over. He seemed unconscious of his virile beauty. It put her in mind of a red kite she had once watched dancing on the wind, so focused on seeking prey that it was oblivious to anything else.

After a couple of hours' digging Claire said, 'It's no good. I'm shattered. I'm just not fit.'

'OK, that's enough for today anyway. We could cut some sticks from the hedges for pea sticks later.' Jake studied her for a minute. 'Cup of tea first, if you like.'

Claire sat on one of the tatty old chairs as Jake made some tea. 'I found muscles I didn't know I had when I tried to get out of bed this morning.'

'Do you want to go home now?' He passed her a mug and offered her the biscuits. He sounded a little regretful.

'Let's have a mooch round the site, and cut pea sticks like you suggested. I only went down as far as School End.'

When the tea was drunk and everything except a pair of loppers and some secateurs had been tidied up and locked in the shed, Jake showed her round the site. The path which they had walked down the first day and the School End lane were the only ways in. 'There used to be a path all the way round,' said Jake. 'But it got overgrown, so now people don't take the allotments. Sometimes we get rubbish dumped, but as the access is a bit difficult it doesn't often happen. Watch yourself here. I'll show you the pond.' He offered her his hand: a warm, dry clasp which sent an unexpected shiver through her. *Careful*, she warned herself. *He's just a friend, remember. Come on strong and he'll run away. And that would spoil things.* Her hand rose to her cheek unconsciously, the tiniest whisper of a touch.

The grass was tussocky and browned by the winter, the old outlines of untaken allotments barely discernible. Scrub was beginning to invade: blackberry brambles and raspberry canes gone wild. 'There's a fair bit of rhubarb which anyone can pick,' said Jake. 'Just grows on the old allotments nobody uses any more.'

'Oh yum. Rhubarb crumble.' *Dad's favourite.* She caught a breath and said nothing for a minute or two. The allotment site was a rough triangle shape, the broadest part being at School End, culminating as the apex opposite. This was where Jake was heading. It was very overgrown there, with a couple of willow trees partly overshadowing a pond, and old spires of a tall weed, as well as something she recognised. 'This is horsetail, isn't it?' She dragged the rough fronds through her fingers.

'Yep. It's because the soil's damp and sour here, or so Ted tells me,' said Jake. 'He says the pond's spring-fed and never dries up, not even in the driest summers.'

'Ted seems like he knows loads.'

'He does. He can be what Mum calls an old curmudgeon but his heart's in the right place.'

'What's this stuff?' asked Claire, touching the skeletal remains of seed heads on the spires.

'Fireweed. Pink flowers in summer. You wouldn't want it in the allotment, though; beastly weed, but not as bad as that horsetail stuff.'

Beyond the pond lay more scrub, and a line of trees. Beyond that were the big gardens of older, large houses. And beyond that lay the ill-reputed Arrandel

Estate, which had been built just after the Second World War.

They cut pea sticks from the scrub and dumped them on their allotment before deciding to call it a day. Jake told Claire to take some broad beans home with her. 'Not much pay for a couple of hours' digging,' he said ruefully.

'It was fun,' said Claire, though her muscles were beginning to rust up already.

* * *

Monday morning there was no leaping out of bed for Claire. It was as if she'd frozen in the night, and every time she moved her muscles shattered into fragments of glass. She groaned. Elizabeth knocked on the door and brought her in a cup of tea. 'I'm off to work now, love.'

Claire sat up, then regretted the move. 'Is it that time already? Jake'll be expecting me.'

'This Jake sounds like a bit of a slave

driver and he seems to be taking advantage of your good nature. Why you should want to help the old chap out like this, I don't know. Though I suppose your father . . . ' Elizabeth swallowed back whatever she'd being going to say. 'It's raining, anyway, and there's some ironing to do.'

Claire subsided against the pillows. 'OK Mum,' she muttered.

When she heard the front door slam she phoned Jake and he said he was going into town for a mooch round the shops and to check out the cards in the newsagent's in case anyone had a job going. He was already registered with agencies. 'Fancy meeting me there?' he suggested. Seemed like a good idea, except she ought to walk in to save bus fare, and just now her legs didn't feel like they could convey her to the living room, let alone to town. But she went anyway. The rain had abated to a fitful drizzle, so the walk in wasn't too bad, and once she started her muscles loosened up.

She caught up with Jake outside the newsagent's, scouring the adverts. His hair was bejewelled with fine drips of rain and she had to quell an impulse to run her hand over his tight curls to scoop the droplets off. He flashed her one of his heart-stopping grins. 'Nothing in the way of jobs, just people offering to do your ironing or weed your garden.'

'Maybe that's what I should do.' Claire cast a doleful eye over the postcards. 'I thought I'd have a look in the charity shops for a couple of gardening books. I realised yesterday how little I know.'

'Didn't your dad have any?' said Jake. Then he winced. 'Sorry, sorry, that was crass of me.'

'No. Dad didn't much care for reading books, just newspapers — the broadsheets — and they took all day to read.' Claire examined the pavement as they walked along. Jake had a chagrined look about him, so she added, 'He learned about gardening from

Grandad. He didn't need books.'

'What happened?'

'How d'you mean?'

'With your dad.'

'I don't want to talk about it.' *Not now. Not yet. Not until I'm ready to.*

'Oh crumbs, I keep saying the wrong thing. My dad just upped sticks and left years ago.'

'I think that's worse, somehow,' said Claire, though at least his father might come back one day, whereas hers was dead, and it was her fault, really.

Jake glanced at her. 'Maybe,' was all he said, but he looked a little better. They were walking, matching pace for pace — close, companionable, but not touching. They entered one of the charity shops and were soon browsing through the books.

Jake insisted on carrying the heavy bag of books that Claire purchased nearly all the way home, then he set off at a gentle lope through the park before she'd had a chance to say goodbye.

Claire lugged the bag the rest of the

way to the flat, slightly vexed with herself for not inviting him in. But he'd grown restive the nearer they were to her home, from shyness, perhaps. Or maybe he was just bored with her company.

4

Claire fell into a routine with Jake, going over daily with a packed lunch. They sharpened the garden tools under Ted's tutelage for the coming season, and started making plans. She could feel a stirring in the earth as if the allotments were shaking off their winter sloth, and she could feel the same up-welling in her soul. For the first time in several years she felt hopeful, alive, and not as if she was just going through the motions of being alive, simply because that was what was expected of her.

A couple of weeks after they started reviving the allotment, Jake told Claire he wouldn't be able to go the following day. He didn't mention why not, and seemed quite furtive about it. 'I'll just carry on without you then, shall I?' she said, a little crossly. So far all she

42

seemed to be doing was digging up weeds. She hadn't decided what to do on her part of the allotment, but had vague thoughts about a wildlife area: log piles, pond, bog garden — the sorts of things she'd been reading about in the books she'd purchased.

Next day when she arrived, she saw Ted was already hard at work on his allotment. He gave her a wink as she walked past. 'Soil's warming up nicely. You know the best way to check?'

'No.'

'Drop your trousers and sit on it. That'll soon tell you.' He chortled at her shocked expression. She wasn't so much shocked at the remark, more that Ted had said it in the first place. For all his curmudgeonly attitude, he'd seemed rather reserved and not one for crude remarks.

'If I try that method I'll make sure I'm on my own,' she retorted, rather waspishly.

She unlocked the shed, put the kettle on and pulled out a chair. She wanted to sit down and think about things; think about Jake in particular. She'd been right about him not wanting any romantic involvement (surprise). They just worked together like a team of two, companionable, but that was all. She loved his shy smile and gorgeous eyes, but she knew she was just a friend. She sighed. It was all she could expect nowadays. She touched her scars and a feeling of melancholy crept over her like a chill. She remembered when she'd finally dared look in a mirror after the hospital treatment. Her first thought had been, *I'll never have kids now.* Nothing since that moment had made her change her opinion, whatever the foolish daydreams.

Stop feeling sorry for yourself. You can't change things; you'll just have to learn to live with them. It was advice she'd given to herself on numerous occasions, but as always, it seemed trite and almost useless. She'd been a bit sharp with Ted, she thought. She made another mug of tea and invited him over.

He sat on the other chair. 'Thank you kindly. Nice to sit meself down.'

'Chair warm enough?'

'Almost ready for sowing in,' he quipped with a wink.

'Jake couldn't make it today. Have you known him long?'

'I've known him since before he was born,' said Ted with another wink. 'I've known Yvonne his mum since she was a tot and Lionel and Mary used to bring her down in the pram. Lionel and Mary came over in the early sixties. In them days growing food was important. Rationing was fresh in people's memories. I grew food and kept chickens in me garden and I had this allotment too. Brought up me entire family without buying much from the greengrocer. Mind you, food was dear in them days.'

Rationing? Just how old was Ted, she wondered. She asked him tentatively. He was born just before the outbreak of World War Two. 'Coolio,' she breathed in awe. That made him over seventy. Ancient. 'Are your family close by?'

'Nooooo, they moved away years ago.'

'So what on earth do you do with all your produce?'

'I sell the surplus.'

'I didn't think we were allowed.'

'I sell it at my front gate. Who's to know where it's grown? And anyhow, it's not like I'm running a market garden or anything. So long as it's genuinely surplus, it's OK to sell it. I got that from the library,' he said with a satisfied nod of his head. 'On that internet thing.'

'Jake's lovely.'

'He's a good lad, not like his dreadful brother Toby. That boy's a handful, always has been. Lionel used to bring him down here and get him to work on the allotment. That helped calm him down a bit. Got ants in his pants, that boy.'

Claire hadn't met the dreadful Toby, and wasn't sure she wanted to.

Next day Jake was back. He greeted Claire with a brotherly hug which warmed her to her toes. He seemed very, very pleased with himself but didn't tell her why. She wondered if he'd got a girlfriend and didn't want to tell her. She kept asking where he'd been but he just laughed it off and said he'd tell her one day.

* * *

The next Sunday Claire's mum Elizabeth suggested, 'Let's go to the garden centre. All we ever do together is the boring stuff like housework and grocery shopping, and I fancy doing something nice together for a change. I like looking at the houseplants and you might get some inspiration for your bit of the allotment. From what you tell me, this Jake is just using you to slave away on his allotment. You haven't actually done anything of your own and

I thought that was the idea. I'm not sure I like the sound of this Jake.' Her mum had a point. Claire hadn't implemented any of her plans, just done as Jake asked; but then, she wasn't quite sure what she wanted, except to be with Jake.

Elizabeth was also right that they didn't go out together often, but Claire wasn't too keen on being stared at. Her mum was wrong, dead wrong, about Jake though.

Claire painted her face and grabbed her new coat and a scarf to hide in.

The garden centre was gearing up for spring, with bedding plants in polystyrene trays, shelf after shelf of them. The place was busy with people loading up trolleys with hanging baskets, compost and lots of trays of plants, even though it was far too early. Claire and Elizabeth ignored the fancy goods and prowled round the aisles of fertilisers and tools looking for something for Claire's forthcoming birthday.

'When I was a child we didn't have

garden centres like this,' said Elizabeth. 'Your grandad got what he needed loose from the hardware store, like a pound of bonemeal stored in big open, rather stinky bins. We even bought broad bean seeds and green manure seeds loose. You could sow some runner beans soon, if you like.'

Claire picked up a packet of beans. £1.95. She bit her lip, put it back and grabbed a packet of carrot seed. £1.49. Some tomato seeds were cheap enough, but others were horribly expensive. 'Oh Mum, this is going to cost the earth,' she wailed. 'And they're just seeds for goodness sake. I never knew they cost so much.'

'There's a bin of last year's seeds going cheap if you want a rummage,' suggested one of the assistants, over-hearing Claire's wail as she stacked the shelves. 'But don't bother with parsnip or carrot seeds because they're never so good when they're old.'

Claire and Elizabeth had a good look through the bin, heads together. Claire suddenly found herself viewing her mum as a friend more than just Mum — a lovely warm feeling.

'Dad — I mean your grandad used to grow these,' said Elizabeth, pulling a packet of broad beans out of the reduced bin. 'And these are the runner beans you need. Now come on, find something for your birthday. I've bought you something special since it's your twenty-first, but I'd like to get you something useful too.'

In the end Claire settled for an electric windowsill propagator. It would fit neatly on her windowsill and she could raise cuttings and seeds in it, just like the books advised.

At the checkout there was a notice board with a temporary part-time job advertised. 'Apply for that,' suggested Elizabeth.

Nooooo. I want to . . . want to play on the allotment where nobody can see me and nobody cares what I look like. 'I won't get it.' Claire knew she sounded like a sulky teenager.

'You don't know until you try. It might only be part-time but it's a start.'

Claire asked for a form and took it straight back to the garden centre when she'd filled it in, though she knew it wasn't worth the effort. Someone else would get the job, someone whose face wasn't liable to scare the customers. She didn't tell Jake about the job. She wasn't likely to get it anyway.

Two days later she got a thin white envelope. *Told you so*, she thought to herself as she tugged despondently at the seal. ''Dear Ms Claire Smith, thank you for your application, blah, blah,'' she read out in a dull tone to her mum. ''We would like to invite you for an interview on 2nd April . . . ' Oh wow, Mum, I've got an interview.'

5

Claire arrived ten minutes early. Another candidate came out of the interview room as Claire sat outside filling in a psychological test. She looked up as the candidate walked past without a glance. She was stunning; immaculate hair, flawless skin, nails the shape of almonds. She looked drained, though. Claire knew then that she didn't stand a chance. A minute later a woman stuck her head out of the interview room. 'We're nearly ready for you. Can we have your forms, please?'

Claire handed them over and waited while seconds the length of minutes slid by. She examined her nails. She'd scrubbed her hands hard but there was a tell-tale ingrained blackness from shelling the broad beans. Maybe she could sit on them and the interviewer wouldn't notice.

She jumped when the woman called

her in and invited her to sit at the desk opposite three people. It was as bad as the interview for the job at the solicitor's. Worse, almost, because she hadn't really expected it for a part-time temporary job. They went though her application, each person asking a question in turn. She had to justify everything she'd put on her CV. By the end of it she felt like she'd spent a day on a windy mountain.

They told her they would be in touch. She knew what that meant.

★　★　★

When Claire arrived the next day Jake was already there, weeding the herb garden by the apple trees, so Claire joined him. She brushed her hands through the herbs and breathed in the spicy scent of thyme, sage and rosemary. Suddenly the garden centre job didn't seem so important anymore, not with wonderful scents like these filling her being.

Ted was right: the earth was beginning to warm up and the buds on the apple trees were beginning to swell. 'My grandad planted those apple trees,' said Jake when he saw Claire looking at the burgeoning buds. 'One's a Grenadier, which is a cooker; one's a Charles Ross; and I've forgotten what the other one is, but it's very tasty. Mum planted the herbs about ten years ago, but they were cuttings from ones my gran had planted. Sometimes I look up and expect to see Grandad sitting on one of the chairs waving his stick and telling me what to do next.'

'That's sad.'

'Only sort of. It's sort of nice, too, because I feel close to him here. Mum makes lavender bags just like my gran used to.'

Claire remembered they had lavender at their old house, but her mum had never used it for lavender bags or anything. A childhood memory of bees busy in the lavender drifted into her mind, and she wished she had something concrete to hang such memories on, like herb bags in drawers. 'This is a very special place,' she said, breaking off a sprig of rosemary to sniff.

'Take that home with you, stick it in water and see if it roots,' suggested Jake. 'It's supposed to be a token of friendship, especially if it roots.'

★ ★ ★

A couple of days later Claire heard the post plop onto the mat, a sort of gravid thud. It was a long white envelope and this time it was thicker than usual. She put her emotions in neutral and ripped the envelope open, let out the most enormous whoop, then remembered the neighbours below and hoped they wouldn't mind. Elizabeth rushed into the hall. Claire flung her arms round her. 'I got it, I got it!'

It was three days a week: Fridays, Saturdays and Sundays. Claire phoned up Jake and shrieked the news at him. 'Well done,' he said in a dead sort of tone.

'I thought you'd be pleased for me.'

'I am, I am. But what if I get a job during the week? We'd hardly see each other then. And what about the allotment? Everything's just beginning to grow. Will you have time to come down anymore?'

'I get a staff discount. We'll get seeds and stuff cheaper. Oh, why can't you be pleased for me?' His lack of enthusiasm was crushing.

'I am. I just said I was. I just wish I'd known. I'd have applied too.'

'Well, I'm glad you didn't, because then you would have got the job and not me, most likely.'

'Not necessarily.'

'Yes, necessarily. Who would you rather employ, an ugly woman with scars on her face or a hunky, good-looking, fit bloke?' Claire heard her voice cracking as she said this and didn't want to cry down the phone or say something horrible, so hung up and ignored him for the rest of the day.

* * *

The next day Claire went to the allotment filled with trepidation. All yesterday she'd been indignantly telling herself she was in the right; Jake shouldn't have been so offhand about the job, not when he knew how important it was to her. It wasn't until she'd gone to bed, fulminating over the conversation for the nth time that she realised two things. One was that a job, any job, was just as important to Jake, who had been out of work since leaving school. This was probably a simple case of envy. And secondly, more importantly, he was worried about losing out on 'us' time. It gave her a glow to know that being in her company mattered so much to him.

Jake was already at the allotment. He walked up to Claire without a word and gave her a long hug. 'I'm sorry,' he said.

'I was an ass yesterday, a self-centred ass. Well done and congrats. Oh Claire, I'm envious, of course I am, but I'm really pleased for you too.' He smothered her reply with a kiss, diffident at first, then more confident as she returned it, totally unpractised though she was.

It was almost worth falling out to get a kiss like that. The heat from that kiss lasted her all day on the allotment, all the way home, all the way to her new job. Because it was a lover's kiss, not a brotherly one.

6

Claire's supervisor in her new job was one of her interviewers. Janice, a woman about Elizabeth's age, was far less scary than she had been during the interview. Now she was all smiles and laughs, and Claire soon settled in. The job was mainly stacking shelves and watering the plants. There were fresh deliveries of new plants every Friday to be accommodated. The previous Friday's delivery would be marked down, just like in the supermarket, until it was chucked out because it was looking tired or took up too much room. One of Claire's jobs was to knock out the old plants and growing medium from the pots and the polystyrene trays to compost further and then be used round the garden centre grounds as a mulch, the empty pots and trays going in a dumpster. 'It seems awfully wasteful,' said Claire to Janice.

'It does, but that's economics for you. Stack 'em high, sell 'em cheap, get the turnover. It's cheaper for us to outsource them and bring them in and throw some away than raise them ourselves and look after them. People want instant gardens nowadays and this is part of it. Goes against the ecological grain though.'

'What's this doing here?' Claire retrieved a pond liner in its box from the dumpster. 'Surely there's been a mistake?'

'It's rubbish, I'm afraid,' said Janice. 'I've just thrown it away. It's got a couple of holes in. Nobody will buy that, even though it can be mended.'

'Oh. Can I have it, then, please? And how do you mend it?' Claire found herself telling Janice about the allotment and about Jake. 'I've read that wildlife ponds are a good idea for keeping pests down and I want to build one, and a bog garden maybe.'

'Of course you can have it. And you

might as well have some of these old plants; saves them going to landfill or compost. They'll either live or die on your allotment, but here they're just rubbish.'

★　★　★

After a fortnight working at the garden centre, Janice told Claire that the personnel manager wanted to see her immediately. Claire knocked on his door, mouth dry, heart heavy. This was it, then: the old heave-ho. Probably because she'd forgotten to apply her camouflage make-up one day and had scared all the customers. She squared her shoulders and waited for the worst.

'Have you enjoyed your time with us?' asked the personnel manager after he'd invited Claire to sit down.

'It's been great, thanks. Loved every minute.' *Don't cry*, she told herself.

'Good, because we're so impressed we'd like to offer you a permanent part-time position.'

Lots of people smiled at Claire as she walked home that evening, and she couldn't understand why, until she realised she was smiling at them: a huge, genuine, joyful smile. It reminded her of her Mum's oft-repeated saying: smile and the world smiles with you; weep and you weep alone. She'd been doing far too much weeping over the last few years. Time to start smiling again.

'That's good news,' said Elizabeth when she got in from work that evening. 'It'll do for now, at least, until a suitable secretarial position comes up.'

Claire said nothing; that secretarial course had cost her mum quite a bit of money and Elizabeth wouldn't want to think it wasted. She didn't text Jake because she wanted to see his face when she told him.

7

Next day Jake was already on the allotment, digging away, when Claire wandered along the footpath. She slowed her pace because he was oblivious to her, focused on his work, his movements lithe and sensual; a moment to savour. As if he felt her gaze he stopped and looked up, his face breaking into that gorgeous smile of his, chest heaving slightly form his efforts. Claire picked up her pace, then stumbled over the grass to the allotment and gasped out her news.

Jake picked her up, swung her round and gave her a smacker on the lips. 'Brilliant news, well done,' he said, setting her down again, steadying her as her legs trembled slightly. They started working, laughing, and joking the way they always did, companionable in the gathering spring sunshine, good friends together.

'Let's go to the pub for a meal,' Claire suggested. 'I want to celebrate this and it's my twenty-first tomorrow. I'm going out with Mum tomorrow evening for dinner, but you and I could go out tonight or the day after tomorrow, if you like. I can afford it now I'm working.'

Jake stopped weeding and stood up abruptly. 'It's your twenty-first *tomorrow* and you never said? You are *bad*.'

'You never asked and I didn't like to say in case you thought I was fishing. And if it comes to that you haven't told me how old you are or when your birthday is.'

'I can't believe it. You're older than I am. I'll be twenty-one in September.'

Claire gaped at him. He seemed so much older, with his rich, deep voice and air of maturity. Not yet twenty-one? Blimey. Now, though, he seemed upset because he hadn't got her anything, and there was a little-boy-lost look about him. 'What do you want?' he said.

'You don't need to get me a pressie. Just come out with me to celebrate.' Claire would have liked to have him come out with her mum on her actual birthday, but Elizabeth was looking forward to a celebratory girls' night out; and anyhow, Claire would have had to explain about how Jake was becoming more than just a friend, and she wasn't quite ready to do that. It wasn't that she'd actually deceived her mum about Jake, but Claire wondered if her Mum still thought that Jake was Ted, an old man.

'How about Thursday, then?' Jake asked. 'You choose where to go and I'll pay.'

'You won't. I'm the one that's working. My treat.'

'Don't rub it in. And you can't pay on your birthday. That would be so wrong.'

'But I want to. Oh I wish I'd never said . . . '

'You think about it; think of some-where nice. I'm off to look for a special

65

person's birthday pressie.' Jake put the tools away then ran off at his mile-eating lope, flashing a heart-stopping grin over his shoulder just before he vanished.

* * *

Elizabeth gave Claire her birthday cards on the morning of her birthday, and her propagator to play with, but as Elizabeth had to go to work she said they would save the rest of the celebrations and the main birthday present for later.

Claire was touched that Janice had sent one from the team at work, and two cards were hand-delivered: one from Ted, and one from Jake. A great aunt who lived miles and miles away had unexpectedly sent her a generous cheque.

Elizabeth gave Claire a hug, then went to work. Claire stood the cards up in the living room, then phoned Jake to see if he was going to the allotment.

'Not today. I'm still looking for a present for a special lady . . . happy birthday.'

'Look, why don't you come over here? Mum's at work.'

There was a silence on the phone, then Jake said, 'I'm not sure that would be right, love. I haven't met your mum and I can't sneak in behind her back.'

'Oh, what? Don't be daft.'

'Speak later, love.' He hung up.

'Love?' He obviously didn't mean it if he wouldn't come over to her house. His excuse was stupid. 'Love' was just a term of endearment, but he didn't mean it in the 'I love you' sense. Obviously. All right, luv? *It doesn't matter. What did you expect,* she hissed at herself. Her hand stole up to her cheek. *He's a good friend, but that's all he is. Don't spoil it.*

Claire wrote her 'thank you' letters and posted them on the way to the allotment. Ted was there so she went over to his allotment. 'Thanks for the card.'

'Yes, Jake told me, and I asked him to take a card for me when he went to deliver yours. I reckon he's very sweet on you, you know.'

'I don't think so. I think he only likes me as a friend, and an allotment friend at that. He wouldn't come round to the flat today. Said it wasn't right without Mum's permission. I think it's just an excuse.'

'Don't be so daft. He's actually quite shy and it's the way he's been brought up, proper-like. A lot of boys would take any advantage . . . '

As Claire tended the plot she thought about what Ted had said. He was right. An invitation back to someone's house when the parents weren't in was asking to be compromised. Jake was too honourable for that. Claire started smiling again and wondered where to take Jake out . . . or rather, where to let him take her out.

★ ★ ★

The special twenty-first birthday present from Claire's mum was a gorgeous bracelet and dress ring (Claire didn't wear necklaces). She put them on. 'They're beautiful. Thanks a million, Mum.'

They went out for a wonderful birthday celebration dinner. When they got back they staggered into the flat and lolled, groaning, on the sofa. 'Birthday cake?' suggested Elizabeth. 'I made it and it's got twenty-one candles on it.' She struggled off the sofa and vanished into the kitchen, coming back with a beautifully iced cake ablaze with candles. She placed it on the table and sang a solo of 'Happy Birthday', then said, 'Blow them out. All in one go for good luck.'

Claire stood up, took a deep breath, approached, then flinched back from the heat, smothering a whimper. *It's only candles, tiny candles. Don't show Mum what you're thinking, what you're remembering.* She flashed a smile at her mum, but could see Elizabeth wasn't totally convinced. 'I need a deep breath for this lot,' said Claire, hauling in an exaggerated breath and then braving the flames with a huge gust from between her pursed lips. Her scars tugged as she pursed her lips to blow, and she clasped her hands together to stop herself from reaching for her face. The last flame flickered out just as the last gasp of breath was squeezed from her lungs.

Elizabeth looked sombre, then gave a brittle smile and clapped. 'Well done. I'll get the plates. Silly me, I left them in the kitchen.' She whipped out all the candles and took them into the kitchen. Claire heard them drop into the sink, and then the tap ran. She stared at the candle sockets in the icing, quelling the racing of her heart.

Elizabeth handed her the knife. 'Remember to wish.'

'Mum, you're amazing,' said Claire. 'I love you.'

8

Next day when Claire phoned Jake she suggested that they go for a lunchtime meal at an eat-all-you-want Chinese restaurant in town. That way the price of the food was fixed (and very reasonable — she could see him refusing to let her pay, job or no job). She would insist on buying the drinks if nothing else.

'Great idea,' he said enthusiastically. Claire wasn't sure if it was the cuisine or the eat-all-you-want part he was most enthusiastic about. 'I'll meet you in the park, unless you want me to order a taxi.'

'We can walk. It's not that far.'

He was wearing a suede leather jacket and fawn jeans, with a white shirt which complemented his skin. He looked amazing, but the jacket was looking a little worn and a bit tight across the shoulders. He greeted Claire with a hug and kiss, and seemed to be bursting with excitement. He was carrying an interesting-looking package.

'Is that for me?' Claire held out her hands, eyes widening.

'Uh-uh-uh,' he rebuked teasingly, holding it above his head. 'Later.' Claire reached up on tiptoe but he held it even higher. They stumbled into each other, laughing. As they walked into town Claire saw people looking at them, but everyone was smiling, so it didn't matter. Perhaps onlookers were picking up on, and sharing in, their joy.

The restaurant was busy but there was a table in a secluded corner.

'Pressie time,' said Jake, handing over the package. 'I hope I haven't been presumptuous.' Claire's heart flipped at that — had he bought her a ring? No, surely not a ring? It was too big a parcel for that. And anyhow, they weren't even officially 'going out', not exactly.

Inside was a beautiful multicoloured pashmina and a jewellery box. Her heart started to thud. 'Feel how soft it is,' he said. 'I know you like them and they suit you.' She held it up to her face. It was wonderfully soft. 'The colours really suit you; that blue is exactly the same as your eyes,' he added. 'Open the box, open the box.'

Her hands trembled as she obeyed. A flower-shaped brooch lay nestled on the velvet. 'It's beautiful,' she breathed.

'I thought,' he said diffidently, 'I thought maybe you could use it to pin the pashmina; you know how they sometimes try to fly away if it's windy.'

Claire immediately put the pashmina on and pinned it with the brooch. 'Wow, that's awesome, thank you.' She stood, kissed him, then nipped to the loo to admire it. When she looked in the mirror she realised she'd forgotten her camouflage makeup, but her heart was too full of joy to care. The pashima and brooch were lovely.

They spent hours there and Jake ate a huge amount of food. He kept taking her hand when talking to her, looking into her eyes with his expressive brown ones, smiling at her. Claire started to believe that maybe they were more than just friends. *Is this real?* she asked herself. *Please let it be real. Please let nothing spoil it.*

9

Elizabeth packed up a large wedge of birthday cake and suggested Claire take it to the allotment to share with Jake. 'Old codgers have a penchant for cake,' she added, handing Claire the package.

'Thanks, Mum.' Claire wrestled with the idea of suggesting she bring Jake home to meet her mum, but she didn't feel ready yet, especially after a comment like that. 'Mum . . . Jake's not exactly an old codger . . . '

'OK, darling. But all men like cake. That and apple pie. It's in their genes. Eat too much and it ends up in their jeans.' They laughed, and the conversation moved on before Claire could back-track.

★ ★ ★

A few days after her birthday Claire took the butyl pond-liner and a book on water gardening down to the allotments. 'It's mega,' she said as she and Jake unfolded it carefully on a grass-covered allotment next to theirs. 'We could make a huge pond with this.'

Jake shook his head. 'Let's just make sure about that. I thought you were supposed to fit the liner to the pond, but we'll be digging the pond to fit the liner — and we don't want to make it too big. Besides, even if we can fix the holes it would be better if we don't use that bit. It's on an edge anyway. Let's sit down and make some proper plans first.' Jake pulled the chairs and a picnic table out of the shed and put the kettle on before opening the book. 'Sit down, woman. You're like a flea on speed.'

Claire giggled and pulled up the chair next to him. They studied the book together. When they measured the useable liner it still seemed vast, until Claire worked out the maximum possible dimensions of a pond using that liner. She frowned. 'That's titchy. I must have got the maths wrong. We'll have masses of liner left over.'

Jake checked the workings out and shook his head, his lips in that cute little pout of his. Claire yearned to kiss them when they were parted like that. 'Don't let's be too ambitious with this, love,' he said. 'Better aim small and do a good job than aim big and mess it up.'

'You can be annoyingly sensible at times.' Claire kissed him lightly as she jumped up to make some tea.

'What was that supposed to be?' Jake was looking bemused.

'A kiss.' Uhoh. Had she made a mistake, read the situation wrong? Perhaps he was just a companion after all.

'Call that a kiss? I'll show you what a kiss is.' He stood, engulfed her in his arms and kissed her a breath-stealing scorcher that left her unsure of her legs. 'I love you, Claire. But now, to work.'

Minutes later they were giving each other unwanted helpful advice as they dug the pond out. For a small pond it took a lot of digging and loads of cups of tea. They made one end shallow, the other steeper and deeper, with a ledge for marginal plants even though Claire knew they couldn't afford any, not yet at any rate. She fancied a pygmy water lily and some irises, but that would have to wait until payday at least.

The sun slunk westwards. The dirt was grating between Claire's toes, and she knew she'd overdone it. Trouble was, she was impatient to get the job done. 'We're never going to finish this today. We'd better fold the liner back up,' said Jake, throwing his spade down with a shrewd look at Claire's face. Easier said than done, and no way was that liner going back in its box, so they stuffed it into an old hessian sack and shoved it in the shed.

Jake sat down and looked through the book again. 'You know what — we can't do this yet. We haven't got a textile underlay or sand to stop stones piercing the pond liner.'

'Bums.' They were stymied. Claire's eyes watered with tiredness and frustration. She so wanted to get this finished. She flung herself down next to Jake. His hand found hers and squeezed. 'And it's expensive stuff, that underlay. I feel a right idiot,' she said.

'We can improvise. We could use the old tatty picnic blanket. And I've got an old quilt at home. I'll bring that.' He kissed her mucky forehead, dust and all. 'Don't look so meh.'

★　★　★

Next day Ted was hard at work when Claire and Jake arrived at about the same time. Jake was carrying a quilt. Ted looked askance at it. 'I won't ask,' he said in the way that hopes for an answer.

'It's for the flower bed,' said Jake. 'Keep it nice and warm.'

'Get along with you,' said Ted sceptically. He gave Claire a quizzical look.

'It's not what you think,' she said, which naturally, sounded like a lie. 'Come and see.' They showed Ted the pond pit without explaining.

'Oh, now you're planting elephants — or is this a cheap route to Australia?'

'We're building a wildlife pond.'

Ted chewed on his reply for a bit, then said, 'Wildlife belongs in the wild. Can I borrow a chair for a sit down? This is more comical than *Last of the Summer Wine*.'

Claire stuck her tongue out at him. 'You could try giving us a hand instead.'

Ted gave an imploring look to the heavens while Jake and Claire lined the pit with the quilt and blanket, tucking the edges in carefully, making sure there were no sharp things to pierce the liner. Jake fetched the liner and he and Claire started to unfold it. The wind caught it despite its weight and it was a beggar to manoeuvre.

'What's this then? A new sport?' Ted had a saucy gleam in his eye.

'Yes,' said Jake. 'It's called pond-liner wrestling. Are you going to help us or what?'

'I'll be the foreman,' said Ted. But he did lend a hand and soon the liner was roughly in place. 'How do you plan on filling that?' he asked.

'You tell us, Mr Foreman.' By this time Claire was hot and crotchety.

'Lionel had a hosepipe when he was alive . . . is it in the shed?' It was, tucked away out of sight, and soon there was a slow trickle of water pooling in the bottom of the liner.

'Take your shoes and socks off and get in there, young Claire, and we'll tidy up these folds,' said Ted. 'You're the lightest.'

The water was cold and Claire screamed as she stood in it. Jake laughed, so she splashed him. He grabbed the hose and squirted her; moments later they were having a water-fight. Ted shook his head in mock despair and went back to his own allotment, grinning.

The pond took ages to fill, and tugging at the folds to neaten them up took far longer than the books implied it would. Eventually, though, the liner was in place and the pond full. They trimmed the edges and disguised them with logs and soil. Jake suggested making a bog garden with the off-cuts, which was a lot easier to make than the pond, as the off-cuts were only to keep the soil soggy and weren't supposed to be watertight. When they'd finished they flung themselves down on one of the grassy spare allotments, grinning at each other. 'That's well cool,' said Jake.

'Well freezing more like,' retorted Claire. They stuffed a couple of old orange nets with barley straw and chucked them into the water to help prevent blanket weed.

'What do you think then, Ted?' Jake asked. 'This will be great for wildlife. Frogs, birds . . . '

'Wildlife belongs in the wild, like I've said before, only you youngsters don't listen to a wise old man, do you?' he told them, tutting over the log piles. 'They've got their own pond over there,' he added, pointing in the direction of the spring. 'I don't know why you want to waste your space with a pond.' But his tone was more teasing than grumpy, and Claire knew him well enough by now to know that his grumpiness was just a front.

Claire took a photo on her phone to show her boss Janice what they'd done with the liner.

* * *

The next day as she walked through the park on the way to the allotments, Claire saw that the gardeners were changing the winter display over to summer bedding, even though the pansies and wallflowers were still in full bloom. 'Oh, that's a shame. I love those pansies.'

The foreman came over and smiled. His name badge said he was Mr Eric

Romer. 'I know. It looks so wasteful doesn't it? And it is, really. Costly in manpower and in new plants. That's why a lot of the park is going over to permanent planting. But people do like and expect the traditional look, so we keep some summer bedding schemes planted up.'

'I find them a bit in-your-face,' said Claire. 'Gaudy — but I kind of like them,' she added, hoping she hadn't hurt his feelings.

'Me too, but I hate the waste. If I had the room at home I'd give some of these pansies and wallflowers a new lease of life. Seems such a shame to throw them on the compost heap.'

'Why don't you get an allotment like me?' said Claire. 'You could plant them on that.'

He smiled as if caught out. 'Truth is, I haven't really got the time anymore. You have one of the Victoria Park allotments, then?'

'Oh yes. I love it . . . ' She rambled on while his team dug up perfectly good plants and chucked them into wheelbarrows.

'You could scavenge some seeds for next year from these wallflowers, and you could have some of these pansies. They'll self-seed given half a chance.' He thrust some plants at her. She fished out a carrier bag from her pocket. 'Oh, come equipped do you?' he added with what sounded like an undertone of suspicion.

'I was going to pick some kale,' she said. 'I don't snitch things from the park.'

'Oh, sorry, I didn't mean it like that. I'm happy for you to have the odd thing when we're changing the display. My team are allowed take things home so long as they would be thrown away ordinarily. Perk of the job, and heaven knows there are few enough of those.'

After that, Jake and Claire often paused for a chat with Mr Romer. He seemed like a really nice bloke.

10

The allotment was planted up for the summer: beans beginning to twist round poles; pumpkins; cardoons; cabbage plants fleeced against the butterflies; asparagus; raspberries which slumped into fragrant sweetness in the mouth; strawberries; salads; beets; chard; and the promise of grapes on the vine. It should have been paradise, but when Claire arrived one morning, a demon was sitting on their garden bench, smoking. Claire recalled his voice and his pig-like squeal of laughter. *If I was that ugly, I'd top myself.*

She marched up to him. 'What the hell are you doing on my allotment? This is private, allotment holders only. I remember you and your horrible friends. 'Crocodillopig,' 'paper bag over my face,' your nasty mates said. And you, you evil little rat, said if you were as ugly as me you'd top yourself. Have you any idea how cruel you were?'

The boy blew out an insolent mouthful of wacky smoke. He wouldn't look at her face.

'See that scar there,' Claire pointed to her wrist, shoving it in front of his eyes. 'After my accident I was in such pain, so devastated by what I saw in the mirror every day, facing skin grafts, worrying about my future, that I did try to top myself. Only I didn't know how.'

The boy stared at the scar, face flooding with horror, and said nothing, but his ears went purple. He gulped a couple of times.

'You said that just to big yourself up in front of a girl,' she added. 'So get off my bench, and shove off, you horrible, worthless little brat.'

The boy stood, his face crimson. 'Sorry . . . I didn't mean . . . And . . . And your face isn't that bad, not really.' He cast his eyes round helplessly. 'This is nice . . . I used to help my Grandad up here when I was little. But he died.'

He seemed embarrassed and apologetic, yet yobbish and arrogant at the same time, as if two sides of him were warring for supremacy. 'And you're a liar; it's not your allotment, so you piss off.'

'You should be in school, little boy. Now will you go away, please?'

He stood abruptly and looked as if about to assault her, but merely ground his sickly-sweet-smelling cigarette out underfoot before leaving without a backward glance. Claire watched him as he disappeared along the footpath towards the Arrandel Estate. Beneath the bench were a couple more discarded dodgy-looking dog ends. She wondered how long he'd been sitting there smoking his vile cigarettes. Perhaps he'd be back. Perhaps he would bring his horrible friends. Claire's hand sought her face; her scars. She'd stopped putting on camouflage makeup when coming to the allotments. There didn't seem much point when only Jake and Ted were there to see. But now all she wanted to do was run home and cover the scars up, or hide in her bedroom. The allotment felt desecrated. *I want Jake,* she thought. *I want him to come and put his arms round me and make the magic good again. I want him to protect me, protect our little kingdom from horrible yobs like that.*

Claire unlocked the shed, brought out a hoe and started savagely hoeing the weeds down. The pond, which had developed into a green soup a couple of days after being built, was beginning to clear. She'd bought some marginal plants at work — marsh marigolds and iris, and some pondweed — to oxygenate it.

Her heart rate was almost back to normal when she looked up to see Jake loping towards her with his gorgeous grin, so of course her heart started to race again.

'What's up?' he asked. 'You look furious.' He gathered her in his arms and she rested her head against his chest, feeling the contours of his muscles under her cheek.

'One of those yobs was sitting on that bench like he owned the place, smoking wacky baccy. I told him to shove off.'

Jake stiffened. 'Which one?'

'The youngest one, the runty-looking kid who said if he was as ugly as me he'd top himself.'

Jake swore and hugged her closer. 'Beast.' He kissed the top of her head, and that made her feel protected. 'He's wrong, anyhow. You're beautiful.'

'You're joking.' She didn't feel beautiful with dirt on her hands and anger still surging through her veins. Crocodillopig.

'No. I mean it.'

'I'm not beautiful, though, Jake. The scars . . .'

'Scars? Stop worrying about them and let the real you shine through. I know what the real you is like and you're beautiful. And I love you, Claire.'

'I never thought I'd hear someone say that, not after my accident,' murmured Claire, trying to add a laugh.

He raised a hand hesitantly towards her face, as if fearing to intrude; then, seeing that she didn't flinch, he brushed her hair behind her ear and, fingers light as thistledown, caressed the scars. 'They don't matter, Claire. Only you matter. And you are beautiful.' He kissed her gently on the lips.

11

Next day Claire could see something was wrong even before she got to the allotment. The beanpoles were down. As she reached the allotment she saw that half the plants had been ripped up. Some had been flung in the pond, but most had been scattered all over the surrounding plots. She wandered round with a sick feeling in her stomach. It wasn't just the vandalism that hurt; it was the sudden feeling of vulnerability. She wasn't sure she wanted to carry on with the allotment if it was going to be trashed like this. She slumped down on the bench and phoned Jake. He said he was already on his way and would be along in a minute.

Claire thought she might as well fish the wounded plants from the pond while she was waiting. As she crouched down to grab them, something rustled nearby. Then something else. Something splashed into the pond and something hit the back of her neck, stinging. A June-drop apple bobbled up and down in the water. She leapt up, looked round. She could see Jake in the distance walking towards her. Her phone went. 'Act like you haven't seen me,' Jake had texted, so she turned back to the pond and fished some more plants out. Another apple hit her back, so she looked round again. Jake had vanished. There was a yell and a scuffling from behind the shed. Then Jake appeared, dragging the nasty little yob with him. 'Claire, I am ashamed to introduce you to my horrible little brother Toby.'

'Your brother!' Claire stared from boy to man and back to boy. They did have a sort of resemblance, but where Jake's skin had a healthy brown glow and was stretched over sleek muscles, the boy's complexion was spotty and blotchy, paler than his brother's too. Both had the same tight curls and finely chiselled noses, but where Jake's lips were finely moulded cushions just begging to be kissed, the boy's were down-turned and sullen and there was no way on earth Claire would ever have kissed them.

'Toby is going to apologise for what he said that time,' said Jake. 'And Toby is going to apologise for his behaviour just now. And the vandalism . . . he's going to put that right.'

'It wasn't me,' said Toby, trying to wriggle out of Jake's grip. 'Let go. You're hurting.'

'I'm not hurting and I won't let go. Now you apologise. You said you were sorry last night when I asked if it was you here yesterday. Now tell Claire that you're sorry. And why the heck did you have to do this?' Jake indicated the vandalism.

'This isn't her allotment, it's Grandad's. She's trespassing. She said it was hers and she's planted all this rubbish on it.'

'I said she could. She's helping me with Grandad's allotment.'

'You never said.'

'I never told you because you'd only want to spoil things, just like you always do. Just like you have just now. You disgust me and God knows what Grandad would think of what you've done, God rest his soul.'

Claire stood gaping while this exchange took place. Toby looked stricken when Jake mentioned their grandad and she guessed Toby and his grandad had been close. Toby seemed more upset over what his grandad's ghost would think of his behaviour than of what he'd said to Claire or how he'd upset her with his vandalism. She wanted to slap him, shake him, make him understand. She swallowed down all the horrible things she wanted to yell at him.

'I'm sorry if you thought I was trespassing, Toby. But really we're trying to keep the allotment nice in memory of your grandad. And now you've wrecked a lot of what we've done. And that's upset me. Just like you upset me with your cruel words that time . . . and you seemed sorry for that yesterday. Shake?' Claire offered him her hand (the one she'd have rather liked to slap him with).

He took it. 'Sorry. I'll put the plants back if you like.'

'I'll be surprised if they survive,' growled Jake. 'But yes, you can plant every one. No, actually. You can fetch them back and we'll plant them. And you can fetch water to water them in.'

The first thing they did was put the beanpoles back up. Some of the bean plants were ruined but most were OK. Toby watered them with several cans fetched from the tap. Claire wondered why Jake didn't use the hose but said nothing until Toby was by the tap filling the can. 'We're not really supposed to use hosepipes here,' explained Jake. 'And he'll wear himself out a bit trudging up and down with those heavy watering cans. He really is sorry about what he said, you know. He has ADHD.'

'What's ADHD?'

'Attention deficit hyperactivity disorder. Makes him fidgety — can't concentrate for long, and doesn't think before he acts. He got in with the wrong crowd and he's impulsive and easily influenced. When he stops to think about this he'll be sorry for the vandalism too. I saw him hiding behind the shed chucking something at you. He was laughing his head off when I grabbed him. Thought it funny, little idiot. I thought he was chucking stones. I could throttle him sometimes.'

'Oh.' Claire could think of nothing else to say.

'He drives Mum to despair what with his smoking cannabis and stuff. He got a lot worse when Grandad died. He adored Grandad and would do anything for him. He used to help him every day. I think that helped calm him down. And of course he hit puberty just at about the time Grandad went into hospital.'

Was this supposed to make her feel

better about Toby? All it was doing was making her realise how unpredictable he was, this little snake that had slithered into their paradise.

Toby gathered up the scattered plants and brought them back one by one. He was as boisterous as a terrier when he did it, and gave Claire a grin when he handed her an intact plant. In his smile she could see the resemblance to Jake more obviously, and she saw the ghost of the man he might become, if only he could outgrow his yobbishness. She told herself it wasn't his fault, not if he had ADHD, but she wasn't convinced.

'Why don't we just plant these where they've fallen,' yelled Toby. 'They look pretty in the long grass.'

'Don't be an ass. They won't fight against the grass. You're just being lazy. Get on with it,' Jake yelled back. Toby stomped over to them, tripping over the log pile.

'Now look what you've done.' Jake glared at Toby, who contritely picked up a log to put it back.

Toby screeched, 'There's a baby dragon! Look.'

There, nestled in the rest of the logs, was something which did look like a baby dragon. It was moving its head lazily. Claire hoped Toby hadn't hurt it when he scattered the log pile. 'It's a newt,' she said.

Toby reached for it.

'No, leave it; you'll hurt it,' Jake told him. 'And anyhow, it's not allowed. I think that's a Great Crested Newt and they mustn't be harmed, or even touched. We did something about them at school — our teacher was nuts over amphibians.'

Toby, on his hands and knees, peered at the sleepy creature. 'Cool.' He seemed enchanted.

'Let's carefully rebuild the log pile around it,' said Jake. 'You watch to make sure I don't put a log on top of it.'

Toby lay down prone and watched while Jake carefully replaced the logs. 'Let's build more log piles. I want lots of dragon's dens,' said Toby. 'They are so cool.'

'Why aren't you in school?' asked Jake suddenly. 'I've just thought. You shouldn't be here, should you?'

Toby shrugged. 'Dunno. It's boring. I want to be here instead.'

'Well, you can't. You have to be in school. Remember what Grandad used to say ... And Mum'll go spare if she knows you're skiving.'

'I like it here.'

'Look, you can help after school, OK?'

Claire pulled in a breath. It wasn't OK by her, not really. She wanted Toby gone and Jake and the allotment to herself, just like it had always been.

'OK.' Toby stood there, shredding one of the desecrated plants to pieces.

'Off you go to school, then.'

Toby looked sullen and rebellious for a minute, then wandered off towards the Arrandel Estate.

Jake gave Claire a no-hands hug with his arms because his hands were covered in soil. 'Sorry Claire, he's a little brat but he's my brother. If we get him busy it might keep him away from those yobs. But it does mean less 'us' time.'

'Hopefully if he's involved with the allotment he won't do something as stupid as this again,' Claire agreed ruefully.

'To be honest, Claire, I wouldn't bet on it, but it's the best we can do.'

12

It was June and the allotment had recovered reasonably well from Toby's vandalism. It was also withstanding a lot of his puppy-dog, boisterous 'help', mainly because Ted had taken Toby under his wing and set him doing useful tasks requiring no finesse in the general grounds and on Ted's allotment.

Toby's suggestion about planting things in the grass had lodged in Claire's mind. She'd read several articles on wildflower meadows and she wondered if they could plant up some of the surrounding barren grass-covered allotments with wild flowers. The bonus would be keeping Toby off her and Jake's allotment.

'Do you think we're allowed?' she added after voicing her suggestion to Jake. 'I suppose we ought to rent another allotment and put the flowers on that, but fifty quid is a ripoff.'

'Let's just do it,' said Jake after a minute's thought. 'Nobody wants them and we might as well make them more beautiful. It'll attract beneficial insects too. In fact, I don't see why we shouldn't start cultivating another allotment and pay up only if the council get sniffy.'

'That's not exactly honest, though, is it?'

'If they didn't overcharge in the first place it wouldn't be a problem,' replied Jake, but Claire could tell the idea of dishonesty sat badly with him. 'I think the wildflower idea is cool though; it'll look wicked.'

So Toby started digging up small patches of the surrounding allotments and scattered wildflower seed and planted any excess plants on these: yellow rattle, which was semi-parasitic on grass and would help the other plants by suppressing the rank couch grass; ox-eye daisy; meadow cranesbill; cowslips; ragged robin; red campion;

foxgloves. They planted small plants raised from seed, and patches of seed, and hoped for the best. Ted watched these antics with a very sceptical expression.

They even planted a few pumpkins on the other, unlet allotments, just digging over a square of soil in the grass, putting a heap of manure with a cap of soil and the pumpkin plant on top. The pumpkin vines started to romp everywhere, but Claire and Jake didn't care because nobody seemed to want the other allotments, so why not make good use of them?

* * *

'How is the allotment?' asked Elizabeth as Claire proudly handed her mum her first harvest of courgettes. They were tiny, the size of her little finger, but Jake said to cut them because it would help the plants get established. Claire was so proud of them, especially as they were early.

'It's great, looking really good.'

'And how's Jake?' added Mum. 'I hope he's doing his fair share of the work.'

Uh-oh, it was becoming an inquisition. Claire had known Jake for three months, nearly four come the end of June; and though she'd mentioned him to her mum, she'd not said much about him because she knew her mum wouldn't approve of where he lived. Not talking about him must have aroused her mum's suspicions about him. 'Yes. He's fine and does more than his fair share. And his brother Toby is helping out after school nowadays.'

'Oh yes?' said Mum, collapsing on the sofa with a mug of coffee. She took a swig, then nearly choked on it. 'Jake's brother comes up after school?' Elizabeth skewered Claire with her gaze. 'How old is Jake?'

'A few months younger than me.'

'I thought he was an old codger?'

'No, that's Ted. I've told you about Ted, and a couple of the people who

105

work the allotments at School End.'

Elizabeth wasn't deflected away from Jake though. 'Jake and Toby. What . . . what's their surname, and do I know them?' Mum's tone implied Claire should have brought them round and introduced them by now. Elizabeth's tone also implied that though Claire was twenty-one, she was still a child, and her mother ought to know who she was hanging out with. Elizabeth also managed to imply that Claire keeping Jake's age a secret must mean there was something seriously amiss with him.

'Handicross.'

'Handicross . . . Handicross. The name seems familiar . . . did they go to your school?'

'No. They went to Arrandel Secondary School. Toby's still there, actually. It's his GCSE year next year.'

The other school. The bad one. The one her parents had been desperate for her not to go to. Her childhood home was in a different catchment area, so she had avoided the bad school, but that hadn't prevented some kids at the better school from bullying her after the accident. Claire thought about what it would have been like if she'd been at the same school as Toby and his yobbish friends, and gave an internal shudder.

'Oh, I must be mistaken about the name then. Where do they live?'

'Arrandel Estate.' There — she'd confessed it. Claire gritted her teeth and watched her mum's expression fade to concern.

'Oh.' Elizabeth's lips were turned down. 'That estate's often in the local papers for some illegal goings-on.'

'Ted, the old codger, lives there too. He's lovely.' 'Lovely' wasn't an altogether apt description of Ted, perhaps, except that under that curmudgeonly exterior he was a sweetie-pie. 'Not everyone who lives there is a druggie or a hoody, Mum.'

'No, of course not, darling. But it must be hard raising kids, especially boys, on that estate and keeping them out of trouble. A lot of drug dealers and criminals live there. Are you sure they're nice people, this Jake and his brother?'

'I'm sure,' said Claire, conveniently forgetting about Toby's deplorable cannabis habit. 'They go to church and everything.'

'And what's Jake doing about a job?'

'He's like me, lots of applications but no job.'

'Yes. But you've got a job.'

'Not the one I trained for. Mum, I'm happy for the first time in years. Don't worry about Jake; he's really, really nice.'

Her mum screwed her lips into a little moue. 'Yes,' she said dryly, 'That's exactly what I'm worried about.'

* * *

Claire and Jake didn't always toil away on the allotments. Sometimes they just took a picnic down or played games. They even played hide-and-seek like kids, and built dens and even a living willow gazebo on one of the unlet allotments, made with willow cut from the trees at Pond End. Toby lost his pasty look and started to fill out, though he still looked runty beside his brother. They laughed a lot.

Ted showed them how to make wine in demijohns and offered them some of the previous year's to try. Claire liked it and so did Jake, but he told Toby he was too young, which made Ted grumble and tell them a funny story about his first taste of cider when he was a boy and how he'd thought it as innocuous as cola, swigged it back and staggered home 'tipsy as a newt'. So Toby told Ted about the dragon in the log pile, which made Ted smile.

Ted remembered Toby and Jake's grandad Lionel working his plot and told yarns about yesteryear when all the allotments were taken and every part was cultivated except the pond and boggy area. 'We used to have a show every year. Your grandad used to always win the longest runner bean, but my potatoes would beat his every time. He came over in the early sixties, if I recall, with his lovely wife Mary. Grand church-goers, they were, immaculate in their Sunday best. Put the rest of us to shame. And I remember your mum Yvonne when she was a tot, helping her dad on the allotment with her tiny watering can. I miss old Lionel. You should bring your mum over to see what you've done some day. And your dad, come to think on it, though I can't say as I know him very well. Not his thing, allotments. Not seen him for years.'

There was an embarrassed silence. 'Dad left Mum in the lurch when Toby was small,' said Jake eventually. 'Mum found it hard bringing us up, though Grandma and Grandad helped a lot in the early years. It got really tough when they passed on too. I'm surprised Grandad didn't tell you all that. Though come to think about it, Mum did tell me not to talk about Daddy

— so I didn't. Perhaps she was ashamed, but it wasn't her fault.'

'Oh heck, I think I've put me foot in it,' said Ted ruefully. 'No, Lionel didn't mention it at all. I just thought your Dad didn't like gardening much. Oh heck, I'm sorry.'

'My dad died a couple of years ago,' Claire said, hoping to break the embarrassment.

'What of?' asked Toby heedlessly. Jake gave him a shove.

'Don't be so rude, young Toby. What kind of question is that?' said Ted.

'It was a heart attack,' said Claire. 'But actually, it was a little more complicated than that.'

'What d'you mean?' asked Jake.

Claire took one look at Toby's interested expression and foresaw him gossiping with his yobbish friends, and shook her head.

13

'Mum would like you to come to tea,' said Toby excitedly one Thursday on the allotments after school. 'Is Monday too soon? Mum has a few days off and knows you can't make weekends, what with work and all.'

'I'd love to,' said Claire, wondering if Jake was actually feeling serious about them, serious enough to show her off to his mum. Claire thought Jake was the most wonderful man in the world, and sometimes daydreamed about the future — their future together. But reality would seep into the daydreams, and she'd reach for her face and guess they were just fantasy. Sometimes she thought the only reason he seemed interested in her was so she would work for nothing on his allotment, but when she thought this she felt mean and shallow for even suspecting Jake could use her like that. She'd looked for little signs that he did love her — and now he wanted her to meet his mum.

'It's a bit of a rabbit warren, easy to get lost over there,' said Jake. 'I'll meet you here at 3 o'clock on Monday and show you the way.'

* * *

Claire wasn't sure what to wear. Jeans? A dress? In the end she opted for a pretty, floaty long skirt and demure top with the pashmina and brooch Jake had given her to set it all off. She put her camouflage makeup on and was picking a bouquet of flowers that she'd planted on the allotment for Jake's mum, when Jake turned up. He looked fabulous in light beige cotton trousers and a black T-shirt which seemed to fall off the cliff of his chest. 'Wow, you look great,' both said at the same time. They laughed and kissed, then he took her hand and led her to the park, where one or two people looked askance at her flowers, perhaps wondering if she'd picked them from the borders. Before Claire met Jake she would have assumed they were eyeing up her scars, and it would have mattered. Now she didn't care what they thought.

Some of the houses on the Arrandel Estate were very well cared for, and most were averagely tidy, but some were awful with junk-like old mattresses and sofas in the front garden. It was depressing because these houses gave the whole place an air of seediness which could easily have been cured with a little bit of care. 'Why don't these people phone the council up to come and take that junk away?' asked Claire.

'Well, it costs money, and these people don't care. Upsets Mum because she remembers what it was like when she was a little girl and people used to scrub their doorsteps in case people thought they were dirty. Everything was spick and span, as Mum calls it.'

Some people had cars in pieces in their gardens, as if they were building them from scrap. Others had immaculate front gardens with neat privet hedges. Jake turned into a house with a wonderful front garden and a fairly new (and intact) car on the driveway. He went to the front door and let himself in with a key. 'Hi Mum, we're here.'

'Hello, hello. Come in, dear. Nice to see you. I've heard so much about you.' Jake's mum rushed out of the kitchen with a gust of spice, grabbed Claire's hand, pumped it, and gasped with pleasure over the flowers. 'So glad you could come. Call me Yvonne. Jake, take Claire into the lounge and make her comfortable. I'll put the kettle on. We'll have a cup of tea now and eat later.' Yvonne was an ample-fleshed and motherly woman as unstoppable as a tsunami. Claire loved her on first sight. Jake ushered Claire into the lounge, which had a rather tired-looking sofa, a modest TV, and Toby sprawled on the floor playing on an

Xbox. He grunted at her.

'Toby,' shrieked Yvonne, 'where's your manners? Turn that off and be hospitable.'

Glowering, Toby did as he was bid. He sat on the floor and eyed Claire up like a baleful puppy. Claire looked round. The lounge was simple, comfortable and unpretentious. There were a host of family photos on the wall over the gas fireplace, and a bookshelf laden with hardbacks, many of which were about gardening. There were also a couple of Bibles which actually looked as if they'd been read and put there for convenience, not ostentation. She sat down on the sofa and it swallowed her bum.

Jake laughed when she gasped. 'It is rather soft and squidgy, isn't it?' He sat next to her and found her hand with his. 'Do you need any help, Mum?' he called.

'No, just coming.' There was a rattle of tea things, then Yvonne came into the lounge with the tea tray and set it down on a coffee table with a satisfied sigh. 'Toby can take the tea round, though,' she said, busying herself with the china service. 'I was saving this for when the Queen came to tea, but she doesn't look as if she's coming after all, so I brought it out for you.' Yvonne chuckled.

Claire was terrified of breaking a cup after that remark.

Everyone in the household drank tea, even Toby, which Claire thought unusual. When she was at school everyone drank pop and implied that tea was for fogies. Claire's mum had insisted she drink tea from an early age because squash and pop ruined the teeth, and Claire could see that Yvonne was of a similar mindset. There was a slightly old-fashioned graciousness about the way Yvonne did things, like the tea tray and posh crockery.

Yvonne saw Claire looking at the photographs and insisted on showing her who was who, which she found utterly confusing. Then Yvonne dragged her into the back garden, which Claire found enchanting. A council house built shortly after the war, it had a large garden which Yvonne had divided up into the flower garden and the rough bit for the boys to play on. 'I might as well make that into a garden too, now they're older,' she told Claire. 'I'm so pleased Jake took on Dad's old allotment. I do like my pumpkins, and you can't buy good ones like you can grow them.'

When Jake had said the invite was for tea, Claire had assumed he meant cups of tea, cake perhaps, and possibly a sandwich or two. What he really meant was a fullblown meal. There was fried chicken, a cabbage salad, sweet potatoes, a creamy rice-and-pea dish in case Claire didn't like the sweet potato, and mango smoothies to drink. It was great and she ate far too much. They talked their tongues to a standstill.

Yvonne offered to drive Claire home, but she said it was almost as quick on foot across the park, and thanks for a wonderful evening. Jake insisted on seeing her home. She wondered if she should invite him up to meet her mum, but he kissed her goodnight at the front door to the flats and the opportunity was lost.

Claire still got the third degree from her mum, of course. What was Yvonne like? What did she do for a living? Was their house nice? Was there something going on between her and Jake?

'She's a doctor's receptionist and she's lovely. And yes, Jake is becoming more than just a friend from the allotments. Mum, he's wonderful. Gentle, kind, thoughtful . . .'

'I see,' said Elizabeth in a neutral tone. 'And has he got a job yet?'

'Not yet, no.'

'Oh dear. Is he ambitious? I mean, is he likely to find anything?'

Claire realised with a jolt that she had no idea. She only really knew Jake in the context of the allotments; they only ever met there because it was their whole world and they needed (and

119

could afford) nothing else, apart from her birthday treat and the occasional foray into the charity shops. Why go out for a meal when a picnic on the allotment was better? Why go to a nightclub to get jostled and pay through the nose for drinks when Ted's elderflower wine or a bottle of pop or juice was nectar enough under the summer skies?

But if Claire was serious about Jake — and her heart told her she was — then she had better start considering him as a provider and a husband, not just a beautiful creature in an enchanted landscape.

14

Earlier than usual one morning, as Claire approached the allotment, she saw Jake on the patio. He seemed to be doing some sort of complex dance with a set pattern of movements. Then, as she reached him, he drew himself up to attention and bowed.

'What on earth are you doing?'

He looked vaguely embarrassed. 'It's a kata. I used to do martial arts. It's like a set pattern of moves.'

'I'm not keen on violence and fighting and stuff,' said Claire. 'What do you want to do that for?'

'It's not violence. It's a sport and a discipline. That's not the same as roughhouse brawling. I started it because I was bullied a lot as a kid and found I was good at it.'

'What, so you could beat the other kids up?' She gaped at him.

'No,' said Jake curtly. 'It's not like that at all. The other kids used to trip me up in the corridors, scribble on my books or steal them, push me around and call me names like 'nigger'. I started learning karate, and they stopped. I didn't tell them I was learning karate, because that's like an open invitation for the hard nuts to try and take you on. But something in me changed; I looked more confident and I stopped being a victim. You should try it. It's great for your self-confidence.'

'You think I'm a victim then?' asked Claire angrily. 'Or that I lack self-confidence?'

'If it comes to it, yes. You keep blaming your scars for this and that, and you won't go places, saying we're too busy on the allotment. You're the only one that thinks anything about your scars. Yes, everyone notices them, but you're the only one who *minds* them.'

Claire put her hand to her face and

felt the polished, taut skin and the tracery of raised bits; felt the tears pricking. She remembered the flash of the pan fire, the pain, the fear. More pain. Morphine. Dad's anguished face and his corrosive guilt until he died of a heart attack, which Claire knew was her fault, somehow. Her mum trying to come to terms with it all; moving from the house to the flat after he died, having to get rid of Dad's things because there was no room in their new home. Claire bewildered by the reasons why they had to move, the resentment of having to leave her childhood home for the flat, battling with the relief of not having to relive the accident in her mind every time she went into the kitchen. She remembered the days in hospital, the skin grafts, and the pain. Always the pain. And the coming to terms. Eventually. Sort of.

'I don't blame my scars for everything.'

'You do, Claire — like when you were looking for a job and you said if I'd applied for the one you got, I'd have got it instead, because of your scars. I bet every time you got a rejection you blamed your scars. It's daft; people don't really notice, especially when you've put the camouflage makeup on. Yet you blame all your problems on those scars. It's like a huge chip on your shoulder. It'd be like me saying I can't get a job because I'm black. Do you ever hear me say that? It's cos I's black, innit? It's cos I's got scars, innit? That's just stupid.'

'No. It's not like that.'

'Isn't it?' Jake pulled her to him. She felt his muscles firm under his T-shirt, taut with emotion. He hugged her close, his lips pressed to the top on her head, and he breathed into her hair, something she loved. He pulled back slightly and she looked up at him into those deep brown eyes. He lowered his lips and kissed her gently. 'Love you.'

Later, after a session of heavy digging, Claire felt better; wearied, but emotionally rested. She asked Jake why he was practicing his moves on the patio in the middle of the allotments. He stopped digging and stuck the fork into the heap of rich-scented upturned earth. 'I've nowhere to go, and I don't want to do it in the park in case some hard case sees me and thinks they should take me on.'

'Can't you do it at your club anymore or something?'

'Not now, no. I'm banned from the local club. I was in a team and we competed at national and international level. Katas, I mean. I didn't like the sparring much, even though it was semi-contact.'

'What's semi-contact?'

'It's where you don't put the full power into a kick or a punch, just touching your opponent, and you get scored on technique and where you made contact. It's safer and nicer than full contact, but I still prefer the katas.'

'What happened, then? Why don't you do it at your club anymore? Why are you banned?'

'We were at an international competition and our team did brilliantly. Then we had a random drugs test — they happen without warning to keep the sport clean. But I failed and the team was disqualified. My name stunk, I can tell you.'

'You took drugs?' She looked at him as if he'd just grown horns.

'No, I didn't. Not intentionally. I was clean of all the performance-enhancing drugs; we all were. I failed the cannabis test, thanks to Toby. When he was at his worst he'd smoke in his bedroom. Drove Mum nuts. She even threatened to turn him in to the police. I must have absorbed some by passive smoking. Cannabis can be detected in the blood weeks after a spliff. I never gave it a thought until I got banned from the sport. Toby felt bad, so bad he said he'd give up. But I think he still smokes it sometimes. Worries Mum sick. She's scared he'll turn into a dealer and end up in jail. And it's even worse for him with his ADHD.

Cannabis affects him badly.'

Claire's mum's words of warning came back to her like cold breath on the back of her neck. People on that estate were often drug dealers and criminals, Elizabeth had said. But Claire remembered how Jake had stood up to the yobs. Then it occurred to her that one of the yobs had turned out to be his brother. Not such a knight in shining armour after all, perhaps; just a bloke rebuking his younger brother. These thoughts rumbled round her head like storm clouds until the allotment work soothed them away. She told herself she was being silly, letting her mum's prejudices about that estate spoil things. Not every person on that estate was a junkie. Not everyone was bad; it was a handful giving the place a bad name. Jake and Toby's mum Yvonne was wonderful, kind, and a church-goer. Her sons were bound to be all right even if Toby was a bit wild at times. Jake was fine. Jake was more than fine; he was fabulous.

And he loved her.

As the day waned Jake said, 'It's going to be a beautiful evening. Why don't we have a cook-out, just the two of us? I bet we've got some sausages or something in the freezer, and there's plenty of salad and stuff. Mum's got an old frying pan she never uses anymore and I could run down to the off-licence if you like.'

'OK, said Claire. 'And I want a shower and things. We spend so many hours making the place look beautiful with all these flowers, but we hardly ever stop to appreciate it.'

She came back to the allotments with some bread and some defrosted sausages. Jake had brought a new picnic blanket which they laid on an unused allotment. The grass was thick and bouncy so they brought out a low wooden stool picked up from a charity shop to use as a table. Jake cleared away some of the grass and lit a campfire. As the flames licked through the twigs, Claire stifled a whimper.

'What's up?' asked Jake, sitting next to her and giving her a hug.

'Nothing,' she said, snuggling up to him, though her eyes were drawn to the flames dancing over the sticks. They had grown in strength and were licking at the logs.

'Liar.' Jake gently turned her chin towards him until she was gazing into his eyes. 'Are you afraid of fire, Claire? Is that how . . . ?'

Jake had lit the fire well and some of the larger sticks were already shimmering with heat, shedding ash with tiny sighs. Claire shook her head. 'It was a pan fire in the kitchen. Dad and I were having a row — I can't even remember what it was about now. I can't even remember exactly how it happened. It's like a montage of photographs. Dad distracted me and the fat caught fire. I panicked and threw water on it. There was a fireball — luckily not a big one — and Dad did what I should have done, put a fire blanket on it. He'd bought one for the kitchen and I knew you shouldn't put water on a fat fire but I still did it. I don't remember much because I passed out from the pain. I don't like talking about it. I'd rather forget, and pretend it never happened.' Her hand stole to her face.

'Shall I put the fire out?' Jake moved as if to stand.

'No. Wait. I can't go through life . . . And anyhow, this sort of fire's not the same. It's sort of friendly, and you're here to look after me. Though I'd rather you cooked the sausages, if that's OK.'

Jake kissed her lips — a gentle, reassuring brush. 'Course I will.'

A few minutes later, after staring into the hypnotic flames, Claire said, 'This place is more than an allotment. It's an Enchanted Garden. The place where all bad things become good and beautiful.'

'You are beautiful and I love you, not just in this Enchanted Garden but anywhere. But we'll call it the Enchanted Garden if you like.'

They ate strawberries warmed by the last of the evening sun, and drank rich red wine as the sky turned inky and one by one the stars came out.

'Can you hear the planets in their orbits?' asked Claire as she lay back with her head cushioned on Jake's chest, looking up into the vault.

'I sometimes think so, but no. Not really.' He idly stoked her hair while they listened to the sounds of the night.

She sat up and rubbed her finger round the rim of her wine glass until it sang a crystal song into the night. 'Can you hear them now?'

He laughed. 'I love it here. I only feel fully alive when I'm here.'

'Me too. I reckon this place has saved my life. I know it's stopped me going nuts. I wish we could build a house here and live here for ever and ever.' She drained the glass and set it back down on the stool, then laid her head back on his chest.

His hand slid to her shoulder. 'Be careful what you wish for — or so they say.'

'Who's 'they'?' she asked. 'And what

do they know?' She was aware of the heat from his hand on her shoulder, filling her with a dizzying swirl of emotion. She moved so that her breast was nearer. Shyly, pausing briefly, he moved his hand over it. Her nipples scrunched almost painfully as she felt a wave of desire flood through her. She rolled over to face him and kissed his upturned lips, unbuttoning his shirt and kissing the satin skin of his chest as she reached her hand down over his jeans. There was something hard inside.

'Are we alone?' he asked.

Claire sat up and looked around. The grass was two feet high, and the night was dark — so dark she could only see the shed and trees as black shapes blotting out the stars from the sky. There wasn't a sound except for traffic far away. The moon had not yet risen.

'Yes,' she whispered as his hand reached inside her blouse. She gasped as his fingers caressed her. He sat, slid his other hand behind her, and fumbled unsuccessfully at the catch of her bra, so she reached up and undid it for him. He nuzzled her and gasped as she unzipped his jeans.

'No, no, no,' he groaned. 'We can't. I haven't any protection. I never thought . . . Mum'll kill me if I get you pregnant.'

'Let's not go all the way, then. Let's just . . . I've never done it anyway.'

'Me neither. But Claire, I can hardly bear for you to touch me. I'm on fire for you; I need you. But we mustn't.' With a sob of frustration she felt him move away.

'I have something,' she said. 'Just in case. I think.' She groped for her tote bag and rummaged around for the little packet she'd been carrying around for ages.

'Are you sure about this?' Jake whispered.

'Yes. Are you sure?'

'Yes.'

His lips brushed her skin, soft as

thistledown, sending shivers through her, and irresistible yearnings . . .

Later, as they lay side by side, still trembling from the wonder and delight, Jake said, 'So that is what the music of the spheres sounds like.'

15

Next morning Claire woke with a jolt. A rush of love swept over her. Jake. Gorgeous, handsome, kind Jake loved her enough to . . . A good job she'd had protection in her bag, buried and forgotten about, overlooked since college when she'd bought a three-pack without any hope of using them, just to be like everyone else — like anyone was going to look at her with a face covered in scars, she'd thought at the time.

Except that Jake *had* looked at her, and fallen in love with her. She gave a delicious shiver and picked up her tote bag, the one she carried everywhere with her. Best buy some more, just in case. But it wasn't the sort of thing she could slip into the weekly shop because her mum would notice, and Claire shuddered at the thought of buying just a box of condoms. That pack of three had been bought when she was with her college friends, as a posse of giggling girls, when she'd tried to fit in, though she'd never really felt part of the group — more a peripheral hanger-on. She fished the packet out of the bag. It was looking a bit battered now. When she noticed the expiry date she went cold. They were over a year out of date.

'Oh sugar,' she whimpered, and went online. A little later she was booking an appointment to see her GP about emergency contraception and perhaps about going on the pill. But suppose her mum found them? It could lead to awkward probing questions, even though she was an adult.

She knew she would have to introduce Jake to her mum at some point soon if they were going to have that sort of relationship, but part of her was afraid because she didn't know much about Jake apart from their joint obsession with growing things. She was frightened that if she showed him off to her mum, Elizabeth would not approve;

136

would spoil it for Claire by being critical. Claire could not shake off a feeling of the allotments being an enchanted place, as if Jake was someone from another world who would vanish like a faery prince if taken into her world.

Claire told herself not to be so silly, and suggested to her mum that they invite him to dinner.

When Claire next met up with Jake on the allotments they were shy with each other, and diffident in the way they kissed, not mentioning the magical happening, but getting on with the work.

Toby came round after school. 'Had another bang yet?' he asked, sticking his tongue out and making rude signs with his hands.

Claire's heart froze.

'You rude little beast,' exploded Jake. 'How very dare you. You . . . '

'What we have or haven't done is none of your business,' Claire ground out from between her clenched teeth.

'Ha, you have then . . . ' said Toby. 'I know what you were doing last night. I followed you and watched.'

'Liar.' Jake spat the word out. 'We just had a cook-out, that's all.'

'Yeah, yeah, yeah.'

Claire was sick.

'You pregnant already?' Toby squealed his nasty laugh.

'Go home, just go home, you,' Jake said to him. 'You have to spoil things, don't you? Everything that's important to me, you have to spoil it. Go home, and if you don't answer the home phone in twenty minutes I'm getting Mum to ground you.'

Claire's head was spinning, and she shivered despite the sun. Hot tears scalded her eyes and the allotments were dissolving in front of her. She didn't dare move because her legs felt disconnected from the rest of her. Jake caught her as she fainted.

'Just go,' he said savagely.

Toby went.

For long minutes they clung onto

each other, swaying with emotion. Not passion. Any passion Claire might have felt was shrivelled up and destroyed by those few horrible, rude words of Toby's. He had spoiled it all, the little demon in paradise.

16

Jake came to dinner in a suit and tie and Claire could tell that impressed her mum. The roast beef came out perfectly, with Yorkshire puddings which had just the right amount of puff, vegetables from the allotment, and even horseradish sauce made from a root dug up from a vacant plot. (Ted had told her what it was. She'd thought it was just a strange-looking dock plant.) The meal was delicious.

Though they had one or two family photographs on the walls, they didn't have so many as Yvonne. Neither did they have a beautiful garden to escape to when the conversation dried up, so the evening wasn't turning out as successfully as Claire had hoped. When her mum's conversation veered towards interrogation about ambitions and prospects, Claire started to think the whole thing would be a disaster, so she started talking about the allotments.

'You should come and see them, Elizabeth,' said Jake.

'Oh no; it's Claire's private space. I don't like to intrude.'

'That's just daft, Mum.' Claire had wondered why her mum had never visited the allotments, never admired her handiwork. Elizabeth was a busy person, but surely she could have found time? Then Claire realised she'd never invited her. 'We could have a cook-out or a picnic; invite Jake's mum over as well,' she suggested.

Elizabeth and Jake ran away with the idea until it was an established fact and they'd even planned when to have it: Tuesday the following week, since Claire was working over the weekends. Jake phoned his mum to check she wasn't working that evening, and the plans were firmed up there and then.

'Seems like a nice young man,' said Elizabeth after he'd gone. 'Pity he hasn't got a job though.'

* * ★

Jake and Claire worked hard on preparing for the cook-out. The untidiness on the allotment which was tolerable in any other situation became an eyesore which needed dealing with. Claire bought some fold-up chairs and a table in the July sale at work and stored them in the shed. Jake scoured the charity shops for china plates and glasses and a stacker box to store them in and keep them clean, because he said Yvonne deplored paper plates. They found a cheap barbeque, which Jake said was a good idea because anything expensive might walk.

Toby appeared with a box of chocolates and an apology for Claire, which she grudgingly felt she ought to accept, though she really wished he'd just vanish and never cross her path again. He quietly (for him) and unobtrusively (for him) cut old branches up to make logs for a campfire. The summer holidays had started, which was a pain because Toby was there all the time. He seemed very excited about the barbeque and his erratic, wild ways seemed to be calming down again.

'Mum gave him a real rollocking,' said Jake to her when Toby wasn't around. 'I asked her if he was out of the house that night and he was, but not out late. I don't think he saw anything. I told Mum what he said and she went mad. But I think she's mad at me, too. I got the 'don't you dare get that nice girl in trouble' talk.'

This hardly comforted Claire at all, mainly because she thought that a private life should be exactly that: private. Now Yvonne knew what she and Jake had been up to during the evening cook-out, even if Toby hadn't seen anything. It sullied what should have been a precious memory, and every hug, every kiss, was now tainted. And what if Toby told his ghastly friends?

Jake seemed to feel the same way, because his kisses were diffident now, and his hugs not as warming as they had been.

★   ★   ★

Barbeque day dawned murky and Claire wondered if it was going to be rained off, but later the sun came out and the day turned into one of those special summer's days when the balmy air is fresh with floral scents. Once everything was ready Claire went to fetch Elizabeth, and Toby brought Yvonne over. Ted looked odd because he was wearing good trousers instead of the cor-blimey ones he usually wore for gardening.

Claire was nervous. Oh boy, was she nervous, but Elizabeth and Yvonne got on as if they'd known each other for years. One or two School-Enders, people whose allotments were at the tidy end by the school entrance, came nosing to see what was going on, so they were handed plates and glasses and invited to join the party. They said they were Geoff and Danielle. Geoff was an elderly gentleman who looked rather bookish; Danielle was a fun and punky girl a bit older than Claire, and a vegetarian, so she didn't have any meat off the barbeque. She was carrying a slumbering baby in a backpack. She told them she kept chickens for their eggs because she knew the birds were well cared for, so Claire knew which was her allotment. The School-Enders were nice but didn't hang around for long, obviously guessing it was a family do. Claire wondered why she and Jake had, until now, largely ignored their presence. Perhaps it was because of the sea of wilderness between their tidy plots and Jake's. The School-Enders didn't feel like part of the magic.

The rosemary was in bloom, and Yvonne encouraged them to use the flowers in the salad. They were as aromatic as the leaves, but with a hint of sweetness. Jake bit off the spurs from some nasturtium flowers. 'It's peppery and sweet at the same time,' he said.

Toby said, 'You're nuts.'

Ted agreed with him. 'Veg are for eating, flowers are for looking at.'

'What about cauliflower?' asked Claire.

'Don't split hairs.' Ted reached for another sausage.

The food was tasty, and evening drifted into night. 'I didn't expect it to get dark. Anyone think to bring a torch?' asked Jake.

'I did,' said Elizabeth. 'And it's late, it's night-time, that's why it's gone dark.' Claire could hear her chuckling.

'Happens when the sun goes down,' said Ted, and everyone laughed.

'I brought a torch too,' said Yvonne.

'Which just goes to show that kids still need their mums even when they're grown up,' said Elizabeth.

★   ★   ★

Over the next few days Claire could tell that her mum was fretting about something. Elizabeth would open her mouth as if to start a conversation, pause, then abandon it. Sometimes Claire caught her mum looking at her, and she'd look away as soon as she noticed Claire had seen her. It was like a comedy, but without the laughter.

Eventually Claire couldn't stand it any longer. 'What's up, Mum?' she said when they were sitting in the living room one evening a week after the barbeque. Elizabeth was reading a novel but had been on the same page for about quarter of an hour, frowning, lips thinned. The rain was slamming into the windows and Jake and Claire had abandoned any plans for working on the allotment. Claire was leafing through a gardening magazine, and classical music was playing in the background. Claire had contemplated going over to Jake's, but she hardly saw her mum now she worked weekends, and Elizabeth worked during the week, so she'd decided to keep Elizabeth company.

Elizabeth looked up and abandoned her book with a sigh. 'It's hard, really hard, because you're grown up now and of age, not a little girl any more. But I'm worried. You seem to be investing a lot of time with Jake, and the allotment has really brought you out of your shell; and in that respect it — and Jake — have been good for you. But I get the impression from Yvonne that Jake is feeling serious about you. Are you feeling serious about him?'

'I love him, yes.' *Oh sugar*, thought Claire, *here it comes. She's going to tell me he's not good enough for me . . .*

'I like him — he's nice and polite, and his mum is a thoroughly decent woman — a lovely woman who I could be great friends with — but what worries me is Jake's lack of prospects and apparent lack of ambition. He's a drifter. And Yvonne told me about Toby being a junkie. I'm worried that if you and Jake decide to get married or something, you'll be marrying into trouble.'

'Mum, we hadn't got as far as that — well, only vaguely. And if we did, I'd be marrying Jake, not Toby or their mum.' Claire could feel her face reddening treacherously.

'Don't be so naïve. You think Jake's the sort of man who would abandon his brother if he got into trouble? I've seen it before, where a family is ripped apart by one member's drug habit. Eileen's son got into cannabis, then crack cocaine. It got so that she daren't leave her handbag lying about the place and he sold her CD collection to buy drugs. And I heard about Jake testing positive for cannabis . . . And I heard the excuse as well, but I . . . They don't change, Claire darling. If he's a drifter now, chances are he always will be. Don't think you can save him from himself, because you won't. I thought I could change your father's spendthrift habits, but I couldn't. Thank goodness he had life insurance, or we'd have had to move to that awful estate, or worse. Even so, as it was . . . ' Elizabeth paused.

'Which just goes to prove that not

everyone living there is a junkie or a criminal,' Claire cut in. 'And Jake was only positive through passive smoking. He's against drugs. You're not being fair.'

'That's not what I'm saying. We struggled hard to bring you up in a nice neighbourhood, send you to a good school, pay for further education — much good that's done you though, eh? And now I can see you throwing it all away on a young man who hasn't had a job since the day he left school. If you married him, what would you live on? Benefits? You'd end up living on that awful estate with no money, rowing over finances all the time like me and your father, bringing up my grandchildren in a place where they're likely to start smoking cannabis before they're at secondary school. You might think you love Jake, but for love to last you need a decent future ahead of yourselves. Don't get silly romantic notions about love conquering all, because it doesn't.'

Claire couldn't say a thing because

tears were gathering and if she'd spoken, she'd have started crying and said things she knew she would regret later. She hated her mum at that point, hated her for saying those things. And she hated herself because despite her heart screaming that she loved Jake, her head was telling her that her mum had a point.

Where would they live? Claire recalled the gardens covered in bits of car, the mattresses, and the islands of niceness in the sea of squalor. They would end up there.

Their kids . . . ? She remembered the yobs in the park, Toby included. Toby, who was driving his mum Yvonne, a 'thoroughly decent woman', to despair with his criminal behaviour, egged on by his awful criminal companions. Toby, who had polluted the magic of her first sexual experience with a few snide remarks.

She covered her face with her hands, fingers encountering the scars, and reminded herself why she loved Jake so much. He loved her, scars and all. She ought to love him, family and all. 'I don't remember you and Dad rowing. Not ever.'

'Rows don't have to be noisy. We rowed in hissed whispers when you were in bed. I gave up work to look after you and that's when the debt problems started. We had less coming in and more going out — babies are expensive. But your father never seemed to adjust; he would buy what he wanted when he wanted, damn the consequences. He was used to a comfortable lifestyle, and because he had a good job the bank was only too happy to lend him money. We didn't fall into massive debt straight away. It was more a building-up of debts over the years . . . living a little bit beyond our means; your dad remortgaging the house to ease the debt. And then, of course, you had that accident, and he blamed himself bitterly; spent money like water on you in compensation — as if anything like that can be compensated for. And we rowed about that too.'

A horrible suspicion grew inside Claire's heart. 'How did Daddy die? I thought it was a heart attack. I thought that the heart attack was my fault, for having that accident with the pan fire, and that Dad blamed himself for what happened.' A bubble of anguish rose to her chest, choking her. 'And now I wonder if he actually killed himself because of me and the accident, and you never dared tell me the truth.'

Elizabeth looked stricken and came and sat next to Claire, arms wrapped protectively around her. 'Oh darling, I never knew you felt like that. You should have said. It was a heart attack, nothing sinister, and nothing to do with your accident — though he did blame himself, of course. His job was very stressful. I think that's one reason why he spent so much money — to keep up with the others, and even as a form of comfort, like comfort-eating — only comfort-spending. As for the heart attack . . . don't you remember? He had a bad bout of flu, didn't slow down, and then he had a heart attack at work. Surely you remember?'

Claire sat rigid, picking over her memories. She'd been at school, she remembered, in the first year of sixth form, a year behind her contemporaries by then. They were still living in the old house. The ruined kitchen had been mended sooner than her ruined face. It seemed like her father's heart had never mended after the accident; not that Claire noticed, being a self-centred teenager feeling very sorry for herself. She'd accepted all her father's gifts as her due, but had never really appreciated them.

The first she'd known about his heart attack was when the school secretary had come to the classroom and asked for her, and taken her to the head teacher who told her that her father was in hospital. He had then driven Claire to that hospital to join her mum in her vigil. Only it was too late.

'I hated selling the house and moving here,' said Claire. 'It was like you were selling all our memories of him.'

'I had to,' said Elizabeth quietly. 'Daddy left a lot of debt — had remortgaged the house, and the life insurance barely covered it. Don't forget that I was working too; I would never have had time to look after the garden as well. And everywhere I looked, I'd see your dad, and remember the argument we'd had the night before.'

Claire looked up sharply at that.

'Yes,' continued Elizabeth. 'We had a row the night before, and barely spoke the next day, the day he died. I sometimes think it was my fault. And now I find that all this time you've blamed yourself. I wish you'd said. I can find his death certificate if it would put your mind at rest.'

Claire shook her head. 'I don't need to see it. It was only a horrible thought I had just now. If you kept the rows from me, I thought maybe . . . '

'I kept some of the details back, darling . . . he was found in the loos in a very undignified state and probably died at work, though I didn't find that out until later, when all hope was gone. And I'm sorry we had to move house, but it seemed for the best. Money can't buy happiness, but lack of money can make you very unhappy. I loved your father, you know. Loved him with all my heart. But he was hard to live with.'

Claire looked down at her hands, digging out the old memories of her beloved dad. She remembered him as a distant figure during the week because he was always home late, exhausted. But she remembered weekend walks in the woods, cutting the lawn, trips to theme parks and the cinema, and holidays abroad, as if he was making up for lost time during the week — and later on, in compensation for the accident. She'd never thought, in the way a child never thinks, just how much it had cost him. Nor just how much it cost her mum. 'I loved him. He was a wonderful dad.'

'Life's a mix of good and bad. We're lucky because though we've had some bad things — your awful accident, Dad dying — we've also had some good things, like the fun times with your dad, this nice flat, your school, your A-levels, even the secretarial course . . . '

'And the allotments. And Jake. Oh Mum, I can see what you're driving at, and I can understand why you're worried. But it's a bit late now. I love Jake. And he loves me, despite the scars.'

'Don't settle on him just because he doesn't notice those scars. You make altogether too much over those scars. People stop noticing them after a while. If he fancies you, others will. For goodness sake, don't fall in love with him just because you're *grateful*.'

★ ★ ★

Claire spent the next few days fulminating over the conversation. She could hardly call it a row; more like an establishing of battle lines. She thought of all the intelligent and reasonable things she wished she'd said at the time.

Toby was subdued, very subdued, and spent his time helping Ted, avoiding Jake. Claire thought they must have had another set-to over Toby's horrible comments, and she wasn't sorry he was so subdued. It made him easier to cope with, for a start.

Jake seemed preoccupied, which worried her. He attacked the soil rather than digging it. He stopped his little gestures of affection; he stopped taking every opportunity to kiss her. Then one day he said, 'I think we should end it.'

The world spun. Claire's stomach heaved. 'What? Why? Is there someone else?' *Someone without scars?*

'No. I love you, Claire — only you. But, can't you see? It won't work.'

'Why not?' Had her mum warned him off in private?

'Look at me. I can't get a job, and the

longer it goes on the harder it is. I don't know where I'm going in life, Claire; not now. I wanted to . . . I hoped that . . . I love you, but if I can't act as a husband to you, and take care of you as a man should . . . then it's best . . . ' He threw the fork down and it speared the ground. Then he turned and walked out of her life.

Claire turned to Toby. 'What's up with Jake?' she asked. Toby said nothing, but blushed as fiercely as he had the time he was sitting on the bench. He backed away and ran off. Claire was left gaping, a feeling of unreality swirling around her.

17

When Claire told her mum, Elizabeth hugged her hard enough to stop her breathing, and said she was sorry, but Claire got the feeling her mum was relieved. She would get no comfort in talking to her mum, then; just platitudes, probably: *There, there dear, never mind. Plenty more fish in the sea.* The worst of it was, she didn't know why Jake had so suddenly left her like that. The scene played itself out in an endless loop every time she shut her eyes.

She tried phoning him on his mobile. She sent him emails. She found she was blocked on his instant messenger, and what really hurt was that he'd unfriended her on Facebook, though his profile still said he was in a relationship, which consoled her until she wondered if he'd found someone new. She tried finding out his home phone number so she could at least speak to his mum, but it was ex-directory. She decided to go round to see him and get some sort of explanation from him, because a nasty idea had taken hold like a bulldog, and wouldn't let go.

Claire checked on a map to remind herself where his house was, then went through the park to the Arrandel Estate. It was about 10 o'clock in the morning. There were loads of cars parked on the road. She noticed that some had tax discs which were out of date. A young man was walking towards her, fit-looking, with a skinhead haircut. He wore a tight T-shirt stretched across his chest and a baseball cap with a rude word on it. He had pale grey eyes which looked at her in a hostile way as she passed him. She fumbled in her pocket for her phone. Down another street she saw a woman in cleaner's overalls staring at her with wild eyes from a living room window. Claire hurried on, her heart beginning to yammer. At Jake's house she knocked on the door and rang the bell, but heard nothing. She tried again. Nothing. He must be out, then, or ignoring her.

After half an hour's skulking she gave up and walked back to the allotment through the gauntlet of tatty gardens and hostile eyes, telling herself that if Jake had been in he would have answered the door. No way would he have let her walk back through that ghastly estate on her own.

After a day's sowing and watering on the allotment she went back to Jake's house in the late afternoon. Some kids on bikes zoomed past, yelling and swearing at each other. The woman was still watching from her window; it looked as if she hadn't moved from the spot and was rooted in place like a weird statue. An old man was bumbling along the pavement towards Claire. She could smell the alcohol on his breath. 'What about it then?' he said, with a suggestive leer. Claire didn't reply but hurried on, nearly bumping into a weaselly-looking lad in a hoody as she turned the corner into Jake's road. 'Want some gear?' he asked. Claire shook her head and rang Jake's doorbell as if she was ringing the till alarm at work. Still no reply. She phoned his mobile again and left a voice message.

* * *

That night in bed, eyes leaking quietly into the pillow, she backtracked over the last few weeks. Surely if Jake loved her he wouldn't have just dumped her like that, with no explanation? He'd seemed passionate enough when they'd made love. He had told her that he loved her time and again, and that her scars didn't matter. But when they'd made love it had been night, utterly dark, two bodies coming together as one — nothing visible, only glorious touch giving each other sensory delight. Her scars were easy to ignore in the dark. The words one of the yobs had said resurfaced; he'd only make love to her if it was dark. Crocodillopig.

She remembered that the following day Jake had been quite offhand (forgetting that she too had been a little reserved). It was obvious to her now; she'd seduced him. She'd made the first move, stirred up his lust until he needed to make love, her ugly scars notwithstanding. Then, in the cold light of day . . . He'd got frightened by her neediness, scared that she would ask him to make love to her again when really, he'd only been obliging her because she'd aroused him — well, her body had, so long as the scars weren't visible.

If he really fancied her he would have found a way for them to make love again, away from the possible scrutiny of the little demon Toby. The thought of Toby watching as she and Jake . . . She felt a rush of bile in her throat.

Eventually she fell asleep on a damp pillow, but her dreams were full of fires and burning.

18

It was hard to concentrate at work that weekend, but Claire had to force herself to; she couldn't afford to lose this job. When she checked the sprig of rosemary Jake had given her to see if it had grown roots, the leaves looked dry and the ends were going brown. She threw the sprig in the bin. It seemed symbolic of their withered relationship.

As the week wore on she worked on the allotment, hoping that Jake would turn up wearing his sheepish grin that she found so adorable. No Jake. No Toby for that matter. She kept calling by his house during the day, but nobody ever answered the door. She'd have gone in the evening when at least Yvonne was likely to be home, but she was just too scared of that estate at night.

Ted said he knew nothing.

A lonely fortnight slid by and she was hurting as badly as the first day, partly because it had been so sudden. She was bewildered by it all. She needed to know why; put the demon thoughts about her scars to rest, if possible.

Perhaps it wasn't the scars at all. Perhaps Yvonne didn't like her . . . Perhaps she'd warned Jake off her. Maybe Yvonne thought her some sluttish strumpet.

Or it might be nothing to do with Yvonne's disapproval, but perhaps she knew what was going on, and would tell her why Jake had so suddenly ended their relationship. Claire didn't know how to get hold of Yvonne because she worked during the day, and no way would Claire go through that estate in the evening. Not with blokes propositioning her like she was a prostitute, or trying to push drugs at her. No way.

Claire knew Yvonne worked as a receptionist at a doctor's practice in the nearby town of Erranby. She looked on their website for their opening hours and location, reassured that she'd got the right practice when she saw Yvonne listed as a receptionist under 'Staff', with the smiling face Claire liked so much.

Claire caught the bus to Erranby. She told herself she was a fool; that this was wrong. If Yvonne had warned Jake off her this could get very nasty indeed. But she had to know *why*; above all, she had to know why Jake had suddenly broken it off like that.

She stared at the passing countryside with vacant eyes until she reached Erranby. Heart thudding in her throat, she took the map out with damp hands, orientated herself, and walked through the busy streets. It was a good day for being on the allotment, and there she was about to make a massive fool of herself.

Claire hung around outside the GP practice building, pacing so nervously that one or two people gave her strange looks. She could see the reception desk through the doors, with a dark figure moving around behind the counter. When the queue died down, she went in. Yvonne looked up and Claire saw a smile light up her face, then die down to be replaced by a wary expression. There was a glass barrier between them — perhaps some patients turned violent, such as junkies searching for a fix. Like Toby, maybe?

'Look,' said Claire. 'I hate to trouble you like this and I'm not going to make a scene or anything, but I do need to talk to you, please. I need to know what's going on. Why . . . '

'I understand.' Yvonne's hand came under the barrier and covered one of Claire's, which were gripping the countertop so tightly her knuckles were white. Yvonne's hand was comforting and warm on Claire's frozen fingers. Yvonne squeezed gently. 'I can't talk just now, but when I'm working late I usually go to the Fleur-de-Lys on the High Street for a long lunch. Good food and comfortable place to rest. I'll meet you there at about one-thirty, in the lounge bar.'

'OK. Thanks.' Claire turned away because someone was behind her. She now had a couple of hours to kill, so she wandered around the charity shops looking at the books, though she didn't feel like gardening anymore. The magic had withered. She fingered through the romantic novels, but she didn't fancy any of them, not when her own romance was so painful. She started rummaging through the 10p basket where the sad and tatty books which nobody wanted ended up before being thrown away. *I feel like I'm in the 10p basket,* she thought. *Cheap; damaged cover.* Then she told herself to stop being so disgustingly self-pitying.

One or two of the cheap books looked worth a go: a very old-fashioned houseplant book, a novel, and a pamphlet on how to write your CV. It looked fairly up-to-date. Claire bought it, thinking that she ought to update her CV, and maybe ought to try for something a little better paid than a part-time job where she would always be reminded of Jake.

Claire found the Fleur-de-Lys early because it was cold and she was miserable. She ordered a hot chocolate and retreated to a dark corner where she thumbed through the tatty house-plant book.

Yvonne came in and looked around. Claire stood up and waved so Yvonne could see her. Yvonne brightened and came over, arms wide, and gave Claire a hug. 'I'm so sorry, my darling.'

Her words were so unexpected that Claire burst into tears. Yvonne sat her back down on the green leather bench, wrapped an arm round her, found a tissue, and waited until she'd stemmed the flood. 'Why has he done it?' asked Claire. 'Is there someone else? He said no, but I don't understand. I thought we were so in love.'

'I'm afraid it's partly my fault, but in a roundabout way.' Yvonne frowned. 'Did you know Jake had applied to join the police?'

Claire's mind did a somersault. 'No. I had no idea. When? He never said.' He'd never mentioned it to her, not once. If he had, Claire could have proudly told her mum he was going to be a copper. Elizabeth would have approved of that, Claire knew — but why was this a reason for him to split, and why had he never mentioned it? Claire shook her head and waited for Yvonne to continue.

'He applied about eighteen months ago. It can take a long time to get into the police. They don't want any old riff-raff, you know. First you have to pass the paper-sift. He applied as soon as he was eighteen-and-a-half, but was declined then — they said he lacked life experience. This time round he passed the paper sift, then he passed Assessment Day One, which was wonderful. He got a good score and felt great about that. Then he had a day of fitness tests, which he passed, naturally. Though there was a problem with his medical, apparently. They take a sample of hair to look for drug use, and that showed some cannabis exposure. And then, before they make an offer, they do background and security checks. Did you know about his martial arts and the drugs test?'

Claire nodded.

'That happened after his application started. And Toby got himself arrested for cannabis possession and shop-lifting just before the summer holidays this year. I was mortified. Mortified. Stupid, stupid boy. He got a reprimand, which is like a child's caution. But the thing is, that all reflected badly on Jake, and the police terminated his application just after the barbeque.'

'But that's not fair. It wasn't Jake's fault his blood test showed positive; it was passive smoking from Toby's bad habits . . . and to terminate Jake's application because of Toby's arrest? Well, that's just plain wrong.'

'Is it? I don't think so. A police officer has to be squeaky-clean, and bad relatives can be a bad influence; can compromise them in their duty. I can see why they terminated his application. But no, it isn't fair, and it was a hard, bitter blow because Jake has always wanted to be a policeman. And then I made it worse. I gave him a good talking-to about you. Told him that if he was serious about you, he must now get a full-time job or go to college, or train for something, since he can't join the police.'

'Couldn't he apply to be a copper again?'

'No. He'd be unlikely to get in. He has appealed, explaining the situation, but we don't hold out much hope. He has to have a massive rethink about the future — he'd set his heart on being a policeman for so long he hasn't even thought of an alternative career. If he'd managed to get a temporary job or two he might have felt better about it, might have some idea what he wants to do, but . . . Well, you know what the jobs market is like . . . ' Claire nodded and Yvonne continued. 'He's been applying for two or three jobs a week for months now, most of the time not even hearing back . . . They only tell you if you're short-listed nowadays.'

'Yes, true. I've had the same. It's bad, especially with email applications, because you wonder if it even got through. It's depressing.'

'Yes. Truly depressing. And that's the problem. He sent off twenty applications after our little chat and not one of them even acknowledged his application. He tried the local supermarkets, but they're not hiring just now. He got demoralised and said if he couldn't get a job then he's no good for you. I don't suppose he told you any of this, did he?'

'No. He just dropped it like a bombshell, then walked off. He won't answer his phone and he won't reply to texts, emails, nothing. I haven't got your land-line phone number, and whenever I went to your house nobody was in.'

'Silly boy. I feared as much, though he wouldn't speak to me about it, either.' Yvonne took out a pen and notepad, and wrote her phone number on it. 'He has been out a lot, looking for work. It would have been easier for him if he didn't still love you. You see, it broke his heart to split up with you.'

'Well, then, why break it up? We were happy. I don't mind that he hasn't got a job.'

'Happy going nowhere. He felt unmanned by the police officer termination, and upset that it was all due to Toby's nasty cannabis habit . . . The shoplifting was to buy more cannabis. It's been tough. So tough, especially with Toby going off the rails again.'

'What?'

'That stupid son of mine is back with those awful louts. And smoking again. Oh, I'm so afraid. I wish I hadn't had to work when he was small, I wish . . . ' The bartender came over with a coffee for Yvonne and another hot chocolate for Claire, unasked. It broke the awkwardness that was growing between them. 'Toby was very, very sorry when he heard that it was his fault Jake's application was terminated. He promised he'd never do it again. Just like he promised when Jake's team was disqualified. But the next day he was at it again. Those awful so-called friends of his. I've felt like reporting him to the police. My own son. And once the evenings draw in, or if Jake does get a job and can't keep an eye on his brother, what then? But Jake needs a job, deserves a job. It's all such a mess, Claire honey.'

'I'll ask at the garden centre, see if there's a job going there. But I don't think so, because if there was I'd have noticed. What does he want to do?'

'Anything.'

'It's all so silly. Fancy dumping me because he hasn't got a job. Why must he be so . . . manly?'

'He's a good boy. He would want to provide properly for you, and that's the problem. He thought it best to split while you're both young enough to start again.'

'But I don't want to start again. I want to be with Jake.'

Yvonne patted Claire's hand. 'I'll see what I can do. I'm his mum, and he always listens to me. Now dry your tears and we'll have some lunch, just us girls together, right?'

Yvonne tucked into steak and kidney pie and chips, but Claire could only manage the soup, though it was lovely soup, rich and filling. She felt it warming her numbed soul as Yvonne chatted. She worked hard, it seemed, for poor wages augmented by a good deal of overtime. Claire wondered how she found the time to keep her house and garden so immaculate. 'It's how I unwind,' Yvonne told her. 'Patients seem to think our role is to prevent them from seeing a doctor, but you know, honey, some of them take real liberties, phoning up, telling us they're desperate to see a doctor, then not turning up. Makes me so cross.'

Claire realised by the end of the meal

that she not only liked Yvonne but admired her, and could treat her as a second mother. Which kind of made it all that much harder to bear.

19

Claire half-expected Yvonne to wave a magic wand and it would all be all right, that Jake would phone her that very night, but it didn't happen that way. She suffered a couple of days of hope and doubt, then got a text. 'Sorry. Forgive me?'

'Yes. I love you,' she texted back.

'Where R U?'

'The Enchanted Garden.'

'B there soon. xx.'

Claire fiddled around with some pruning on the allotment, waiting for Jake. She looked up to see Jake walking down the path rather diffidently. She rushed to the shed, put the secateurs down, tore off her gloves, ran over to him, and threw herself into his arms. He felt stiff and unresponsive, then melted into her. She found she was crying.

'Mum gave me a right old rollicking,' he said ruefully. 'I thought I was doing the right thing, Claire my love. I thought I was on the scrap heap and that nobody wanted me.'

'I want you.'

'I know. I meant job-wise though. Mum told you about the police?'

'Yes. That's so unfair.'

'I was gutted, Claire, gutted. And all because of my stupid kid brother. I wish . . . I wish he'd grow up.'

'Me too. I can't believe you're brothers. You're so nice, and he's an utter pillock.'

'He's got ADHD, remember. He sometimes doesn't think things through. Impulsive. And often the impulses are the wrong ones. He's smoking skunk again. Mum wants him to go to the doctor's — says the skunk's making his ADHD worse — but he won't go. Short of tying him up and dragging him there, I don't know what we can do. And Mum's wary of the medication too, and I reckon Toby's only pretending to take it. We're so worried.'

Claire remembered what her mum had said about marrying into problems. It was obvious that she had a point. But Claire loved Jake and if she wanted him, his wretched brother was a price she'd have to pay. She shivered.

'But I have got some good news. I've got a job. A proper job.'

'Great. Coolio. What?' Claire smiled so wide it hurt.

'Selling burglar alarms. I get a van and everything.' Jake looked ecstatic.

'I didn't know you can drive.'

'Yeah. Passed when I was eighteen. First time. But I can't afford a car because the insurance is horrendous. This is a great opportunity, Claire. I get a basic wage and commission on top. I have a week's training and then I start.'

'Oh.' Uh-oh. Sales. Claire had heard stories about dodgy salesmen. She couldn't see Jake as one, but she didn't dare say anything negative because she didn't want to break this fragile reconciliation. He'd only come to see her, to make up with her, once he had a job snagged. If he lost it, she might lose him again. But she was worried. 'Do you have to go round selling them like a door-to-door salesman?'

'No, that's done over the phone. I go round and clinch the deal. Then the techies go and fit the burglar alarm. It's all aboveboard.' He sounded enthusiastic, but that last comment revealed that he too had doubts.

Claire lit the stove and put the kettle on. Jake got out two of the chairs and they sat holding hands and talking about the future until the sun went down. Claire told Jake about how there didn't seem to be any existence with him outside the allotments; how it felt as if it was an enchantment in a fairy story, a fantasy. 'It's almost as if when we try to be together outside the Enchanted Garden it all goes wrong,' she said with a rueful laugh.

'I'll take you out properly when I'm earning, I promise you. We do go into town sometimes, though, so it's not just here.'

'That wasn't quite what I meant,' said Claire. 'Not exactly. But it will be nice to go out and do different things together rather than just gardening or shopping for gardening books. We must save for the future, but I could take you out — for a meal perhaps, to celebrate your new job. I owe you for my birthday.'

'I don't know . . . '

'Why not? We agreed to go Dutch all those months ago, remember. What's wrong with me taking you out?'

'A bloke doesn't live off his girlfriend. It's not right.'

'Oh don't be so . . . nineteenth century. Of course they do.'

'I'll walk you home.' He had a torch, which was just as well as it was a stiflingly dark night. He kissed her goodbye outside the flats. It was passionate, meaningful and reassuring.

⋆   ⋆   ⋆

Over the next couple of days they exchanged lots of loving texts and emails and he phoned her every day. The first day of his new job he was filled with enthusiasm. It had been a day's training on the burglar alarm itself. He raved about it and said he might get one for his mum. But by Wednesday he was conspicuously silent about what he'd learned. 'What's the matter?' asked Claire.

'Not sure. Just got a dodgy feeling about all this. Thing is, Claire, we sell the system for a pittance, but we sell the maintenance contract for a lot — and I mean a lot of money, and we only tell the customer about that when we go to clinch the deal ... my job. And we're not supposed to take 'no' for an answer. That's pressure sales, and that's ... well, I think it's illegal.'

'Oh. Well if it's not for you, then tell them to shove it.'

'Don't be daft. I need this job.'

Thursday when he phoned he was even more to the point. 'I went out with one of their regular sales people today. You know what I have to do? Go to someone's home, make them deadly scared about the level of crime in the area by quoting figures and showing them a video about broke-into homes — burglars can make a hell of a mess, trash the place — then offer them the cut-price burglar alarm. Then, just as they're feeling safe again, hit them with a five-year minimum maintenance contract, paid monthly so they can 'afford' it. We say it's approved by the police — and that's not true, not exactly. And if they still don't sign we send a silent text to the boss sitting in his office. He then phones us to 'see how things are going' and we explain that the client can't afford it, so he says just give them the burglar alarm for free, but with the maintenance contract of course. Then if they still won't bite he'll tell us to offer a special price just for them, just on the day, and that is high-pressure sales. It's a crock of poo and I hate it, Claire. It's wicked. I wanted to spend my life protecting people, not scamming them.'

'The salesmen can't all be like that, surely? This must be a one-off if it's illegal. Just that salesman.'

'No, because he's their top salesman and he's the one who gives us the training.'

'Surely not every company is like that, though? Some must trade honestly. What's the company's name?'

Jake told her. It sounded very like a name she'd heard on the TV and radio. 'I'm going to do some digging on the internet. Why don't you just jack it in?'

'But I need this job. For us.'

'It's not worth it. And I can't see you being successful anyway. You're too honest.'

Jake sounded tortured. Claire felt a qualm — if he did jack it in, would he leave her again, or was that silliness now in the past?

20

After Jake hung up, Claire went online and searched for a mention of this company. She found out that it was a very young company that had only been trading a couple of months, and that the director was the MD of another company which had been selling a different brand of burglar alarm. She googled that brand and came across a forum for disgruntled customers complaining about the same sales tactics. She printed a few things out but didn't phone Jake because it was very late, and instead sent him a text and an email with the links and some of the complaints. She also found a legitimate company with a similar-sounding name, the one whose adverts she vaguely remembered seeing and hearing. It looked like the company Jake was working for was trying mimicry of the legitimate one. Claire decided to phone the legitimate company up the next day and ask them about burglar alarms, and to phone Trading Standards to see what they had to say.

But the next morning she had doubts. Jake wanted this job and if she phoned Trading Standards they might make him lose it. So she phoned up the different, legitimate burglar alarm company and they told her the deal over the phone; no need to send a salesman round. And their prices for their maintenance contract were far more competitive than the company Jake was working for. It looked very dodgy, but Claire still didn't dare phone Trading Standards; she went to the allotment and wrestled with her conscience instead. She was just about to go home for a late lunch when she saw Jake walking towards her. She ran to him and he caught her in his arms, kissed her briefly and sighed. 'I'm now unemployed again.'

'Good . . . you got my email?'

'I got your text but I didn't have time to log onto my computer.'

'Oh, well that firm is dodgy, very dodgy; real rip-off merchants. Did they sack you?'

'I walked out. And I'm going to the Job Centre to tell them exactly why. You know I'm not yet twenty-one?'

'Yes. Coming up soon though, isn't it? You must let me take you out for that.'

'Mum's planning a humongous party. Anyway, you know I said about getting a van and everything? I asked to see the company insurance policy, basically because I was beginning to think the whole set-up was dodgy. The policy only covers those over twenty-five. So I said I couldn't drive the van, and the sales bloke, the one I went out with, said it didn't matter, just drive it and don't say anything. No way, I said. Not unless I'm insured. So they said use my own car, but I don't have one. So they said drive the van or nothing. So I said nothing. So here I

189

am. Jobless. Oh Claire, I was so excited for us, and now . . . '

Claire saw his jaw working as he looked away into the distance. 'You did absolutely the right thing,' she said, giving him a hug, 'and I hope that company gets what's coming to them. Bunch of criminals. You should report it to the police. One of the reasons I love you so much is because you're so honest and noble.' At last she saw that grin she loved so much, the flash of the eyes, the bashful smile blossoming into a big grin. 'And I love you.'

★　★　★

Claire prayed Yvonne would answer the phone and not Jake or Toby, and her prayers were answered. 'Hi, Yvonne, it's Claire here. I want to get Jake a nice birthday pressie, and I might get him a shirt or something; not sure. But I don't actually know his size.'

Yvonne told her and mentioned that she'd got him a quality watch, shirt and tie and a suit, so that Claire didn't duplicate gifts, adding that she hadn't a clue what Toby was getting for Jake, though she had given him £10 to spend. 'I don't give him pocket money as a rule now,' she confided. 'He'll only spend it on the wrong things.' They discussed the birthday party Yvonne was going to host in a couple of day's time. Claire could tell she was really excited.

Next day Claire told Jake she wouldn't be over on the allotments that day, and wandered into town. It was harder than she thought, shopping for something special. She wondered about some bling, but Jake wasn't a very blingy sort of bloke. A watch was a good choice, but his mum was getting that. Eventually she found an awesome leather jacket which she knew would look great on him, and though it was expensive, it was good value.

She spent ages in the card shop trying to find a card that she liked. She could have gone home then, but she really fancied a good relaxing mooch round the shops now she'd got what she needed. Jake would have laughed and said that shopping was a girl-thing. She looked in the estate agent's window, just out of interest. The house prices were shocking. Perhaps she could look online when she got home, and see if there was anything cheaper. Not that she was planning on buying anything, but it was nice to daydream about it.

In a bargain bookshop she found a book on wildlife gardening that would do as an extra present for Jake. She also found a gardening book aimed at young adults and wondered if Toby would like it. The pictures were big and clear, with lots of them, and the text was in short enough chunks for someone who couldn't concentrate for long to cope with. She'd looked up ADHD on the internet and found out some of the symptoms, like a lack of concentration (yep), impulsiveness (yep), risk-taking (yep), and learning problems (yep). Toby didn't deserve a present — he so did not deserve one — but it was reasonably priced and Claire thought he might feel left out if Jake was centre of attention, so she bought it for him, thinking it was like mollifying a toddler.

As if thinking about Toby had materialised him out of thin air, she saw him with a group of teenagers draping themselves over the seats in the pedestrianised precinct. Toby was smoking, and Claire suspected it was cannabis. *Idiot*, she thought. She recognised a couple of the other kids as being the yobs who had mocked her in the park. The girl had body-piercings now, and wore a perpetual sneer which did nothing for her looks. Claire saw Toby hastily stub out his spliff, crushing it into the plant tub behind the seats. A copper was walking along the pavement. As a single entity the brat-pack stood up, sauntered off and vanished into a department store.

Claire followed them at a distance, thumbs pricking. They were poring over fancy goods en masse. She didn't like the way they were standing, or the way they were moving. It looked dodgy. Toby and the girl broke off from the group and left the shop. Claire followed and saw them look round before sitting back down, bags on their laps. They were laughing together. They parted and Toby started walking in the direction of home.

A hundred yards later Claire caught up with him. 'Hi Toby,' she said, a shade too jovially. 'Haven't seen you on the allotments for a while. Do you go at the weekend while I'm at work?'

He looked shifty, distinctly shifty. He looked straight at her and said earnestly, 'I'm too busy with my homework now. GCSEs.'

'Good for you,' said Claire, hating herself because she sounded just like her mum's friends used to when she was still at school, being quizzed about her favourite lessons. The pair of them

194

walked on together in uneasy silence until the road divided and she said, 'Bye, see you tomorrow at the party.'

He grunted an incomprehensible reply.

21

'We'll take a taxi,' said Elizabeth. She looked wonderful in a casual evening-wear designer dress cut on the bias, which clung to her hips. It managed to look classy and sexy at the same time. She took a stole in case it turned chilly later on. Claire decided on a classic black evening dress that she'd had since the prom at school. She wore her birthday bracelet.

Elizabeth had a little package for Jake. 'I hope he likes it,' she said. 'It's difficult enough to buy for boys at the best of times, and I feel like I hardly know him.'

Claire wasn't sure whether to take that as a rebuke or not. 'I invited him over ages ago but he wouldn't come until he'd met you properly, and I never thought to invite him over again. I ought to now winter's coming.'

'He wouldn't come over? Whyever not?'

'Said it wasn't proper, not without your permission.' Claire could see this answer pleased her mum.

'You'll have to invite him for another meal. I think I need to get to know him.'

Elizabeth's lips turned down as she stared out of the taxi window at the shabby estate where Jake lived. Claire said nothing, either.

Jake opened the door. 'Wow, Elizabeth, you look amazing. I can see where Claire gets her gorgeous figure from. Come in.'

Yvonne bustled through and greeted them with a kiss. 'Oh, look at you both. Come in, sit down and have a cup of tea. We invited you early because you're practically family and we thought you'd like to see Jake open his presents.'

Elizabeth gave Claire a penetrating look, as if Claire had neglected to tell her something. They sat down in the lounge, and once the tea was poured,

Jake opened his presents. He smiled over the suit, shirt and tie, fingering the material. 'I'll look the business in this, Mum. Thanks.'

Toby gave him a gentleman's gift set of wallet, key ring and pen, just like the ones Claire had seen Toby looking at the evening before in the department store. Jake smiled. 'Oh wow, Toby. That's great. Thanks.'

Claire handed him her gifts. He unwrapped the book first, and flicked through. 'Great,' he said, turning to the bigger parcel, feeling it through the paper with that lovely grin of his. He tore the paper off and shook the jacket out. 'Wicked.' He put it on and he looked awesome in it. 'Oh yes, who's the daddy.'

'Not you, not yet a while I hope, young man,' teased Yvonne.

'Well . . . ' said Toby, so Claire hurriedly handed Toby his gift.

'It's just a little something,' she said. 'When I was shopping I saw this and thought of you.'

'Aw wicked, thanks.' He unwrapped it and flicked though it. 'It's great, thanks. Hey Ted, it's got how to make bat boxes and bird boxes in it and stuff like that, as well as gardening. Wicked.'

'Bats,' said Ted with a roll of his eyes. He gave Jake a small parcel. It was a digital camera. Jake looked at it, and looked at Ted. 'I've wanted one of these for ages . . . How did you know?'

'Oh, a little bird told me.'

Jake looked at Claire and she shook her head. 'Not me.'

Elizabeth gave Jake some cufflinks, really classy ones. His mouth quirked into Claire's favourite smile. 'They're great,' he said. 'Thank you.'

'Go and put your suit on; let's see you all togged up,' said Yvonne. Five minutes later he was back downstairs. Claire's heart swelled. He looked really cool. He admired the cufflinks in the shirt which was just peeping from the jacket perfectly. 'It's awesome. I'll wear all this to my next interview. If I ever get one.'

'Go and change back out of it and keep it nice then,' suggested Yvonne.

Other people started arriving and the party got underway. They spilled out into the garden, and danced as the sun went down. Jake danced with Claire whenever he wasn't talking with people. Mum helped Yvonne in the kitchen and they seemed to spend the whole evening talking. Ted's face grew rosier and rosier and his jokes got cruder as the evening wore on.

When Elizabeth and Claire got home Elizabeth said, 'I am stuffed to the gills. I couldn't eat another thing. That was a great party. I wish I'd done something like that for yours.' She looked regretful.

'Mum, I had a lovely meal out with you, and it's all I wanted or needed.'

'Jake is a nice young man. You should invite him round more often.'

'Thanks, Mum. I wasn't sure how you'd take to him.'

'I can see why you love him, and Yvonne and I are going to be good friends, I can see that. I was a bit shocked when Yvonne said we were practically family, though.'

'So was I,' Claire giggled. 'I thought perhaps Jake had proposed and I hadn't noticed.'

'Umn . . . ' agreed Elizabeth. 'Yvonne told me he's still after a job, and about the problem with his police application. I wish I'd known about it; I wouldn't have thought him such a drifter.'

'He didn't tell many people in case it all went wrong. Besides, on that estate wanting to be a copper isn't something you confess to. So he kept it quiet, even from me.'

'That Toby is trouble, though, but that was a kind thought about the book for him, Claire.'

'Maybe. He's such a pain, though.'

* * *

That night, as Claire lay in bed with sleep eluding her, she pondered over the lovely gift Toby had bought for Jake.

201

Had he really bought it, or had he spent the money Yvonne had given him on cannabis, and nicked the present in front of her eyes? She recalled the milling brat pack and the gleeful body language of Toby and the girl once they'd gone outside the store.

The next three days Claire was at work, and in the quieter moments the idea niggled at her. Yvonne had told her that Jake had appealed the decision to terminate his application for the police. That appeal was still ongoing as far as Claire knew, though Jake didn't hold out much hope. If Toby were to be nicked for shoplifting again, then that would put the kybosh on any hope of success for Jake's appeal.

On Tuesday at the Enchanted Garden, she told Jake what she'd seen. 'Sorry to spoil things with my suspicions,' she said. 'And I could be wrong. He was looking at them in the shop the night before last. He could have gone back during the day to buy it for you.'

'I think you and I need to have a

chat with Mum about this, because I walked with Toby to school and met up with him after school the day of my birthday. I don't think he'd have had an opportunity to buy it.'

'Lunchtime, perhaps?'

Jake shrugged. 'Maybe.'

Just then Ted arrived. Jake went over and pulled an envelope from his pocket. 'It's a thank-you letter, Ted. I can't believe you knew I wanted a camera.'

'Young Toby told me. Even said he would get it for me if I just gave him the money.'

Claire felt a sick, sinking sensation. 'Did he give you a receipt or just the camera?' she asked.

'He said he lost the receipt. He's such a scatterbrain.' Ted looked from Claire to Jake and back to Claire. 'What's the matter?'

22

Toby was in the lounge lolling on the floor, playing on the Xbox, when Claire and Jake went in. Ted followed and sat down on the sofa, looking startled as he sunk into it. Toby was too engrossed to notice. Then Yvonne sat down next to Ted. Jake closed the door, sat down and leaned against it. Claire sat in the armchair.

'Toby, stop playing that game. We need to talk.' Yvonne's tone was firm but sad.

'In a minute,' said Toby without looking round at her.

'No, now,' said Ted.

Toby twisted round and dropped the control box. 'What? What's up?'

'When did you buy that cool present you gave me, Toby?'

'Thursday afternoon.' The day Claire had seen him in town with the yobs.

'Have you got the receipt, please?' said Jake.

'Why? If I give you the receipt you'll know what I paid for it. It's a present.'

'Then give Mum the receipt please, Toby.'

'I threw it away.'

'What time did you buy it?' asked Claire. Her heart was thudding into her ribs. She was hating this, but not as much as Yvonne was, judging by her expression.

'Dunno.'

'And where did you get the camera? I need the receipt to activate the guarantee.'

Toby sat there gawping like a stranded goldfish. Claire told him what she'd seen on Thursday afternoon. Jake reminded Toby he'd been with him all Thursday evening.

'I bought it lunchtime at school on your birthday.'

'That's odd,' said Yvonne, 'because when I asked the school I was told you had a lunchtime detention then.'

'You stole them, didn't you Toby?' said Ted quietly. 'And you took my money and pretended that was to buy the camera. Whatever would your grandad think of you now? That's shameful.'

Toby burst into tears. 'No I didn't.'

'You've spoiled it,' Jake said. 'You've spoiled my birthday. You wrecked my sporting future, you wrecked my hopes of joining the police, and you've even spoiled my twenty-first birthday.' Jake's voice was soft, his tone wondering, as if he couldn't quite believe it. Claire swallowed hard.

'I've a good mind to hand you to the police myself,' said Yvonne. 'My own son, my own flesh and blood.'

'I'm sorry. I'm sorry, Mummy.' Toby started rocking to and fro.

'But you're not, though, are you?' said Ted. 'Your 'sorry' only lasts as long as you're in trouble, or you wouldn't keep doing it. This is it, chum. Your wake-up call.'

'Right,' said Yvonne, pulling out a

sheet of paper with a list of rules. 'This is what's going to happen. You and I will take these goods back to the shops and you will apologise to the managers . . . If they want to take it up with the police you'll end up arrested and will have to face the consequences. If you get lucky and the managers are forgiving, you are grounded except to go to school. You will sign into each lesson with your teachers . . . and I have arranged this already. You will be in lunchtime detention indefinitely, and after school you will be met by Ted or Jake or Claire. You will either go with them and work on the allotment or come home immediately and be baby-sat by one of them. You will take your ADHD medication in front of witnesses. And your teachers have been advised that you are not allowed fizzy drinks of any description, just the packed lunch I prepare for you. You will do all of this or I will turn you in to the police myself. I can't let you become an adult criminal. I really can't. You either agree now or we phone the police. Which is it to be?' Yvonne was holding the phone up, ready to dial.

'Don't turn me in.' Toby sounded disbelieving and looked around at everyone, jaw slack, tears draining down his face.

'So sign this,' Yvonne said.

He signed.

23

Toby was forced to give Ted back the money he had been given to buy the camera, and Ted gave it to Yvonne on the sly so that when Yvonne took Toby to the camera shop, she bought a different camera for Jake. The manager was very kind about it all, Yvonne told Claire later, though he gave Toby a quiet but stern talking-to about what theft like that meant to his business. The department store manager wasn't quite so nice about it, but didn't call the police. 'You're a lucky boy to have a mum like yours,' she said. 'I don't want to see you in the store again. You are banned. As are your friends, and I know who they are.'

* * *

A few weeks later Claire and Jake were cuddling on the sofa and Toby was fulminating over his homework when Yvonne arrived home. There was a letter waiting for her and they all knew it was from the school because there was a school crest stamped on the front. Jake jumped up to make his Mum a cup of coffee while she sat down and looked despairingly at the envelope. Toby was suddenly very engrossed in his homework.

Yvonne peeled the envelope open and scanned the contents, then her facial expression relaxed as she took her time over reading it properly. She read it aloud.

'Dear Mrs Handicross,

We are delighted to tell you that recently Toby's work has improved beyond all recognition. His marks are improving, but perhaps more importantly, he seems far more settled and focused in class. His predicted grades have improved, and if he continues to improve at this pace we are hopeful of at least five reasonable passes at

GCSE. We do hope Toby remains focused, because though we have seen improvement there is still a long way to go.

The lunchtime detentions seem to be working well. Toby spends his time with Mr Thomkins, the woodwork teacher, making bird boxes and bat boxes, something he is really enjoying, which is good because 'detention' of this nature should not be seen as a punishment. Perhaps 'distraction' is a better term. Toby says they are for the allotments. Toby often talks about the allotments, and seems to be very keen on the work he does there. In fact, the other day he gave a PowerPoint presentation to his form in their Personal Development class, with photographs taken on the allotment. For Toby this is a very creditable achievement.

All in all we, his teachers, feel that this intensive strategy of help is working for Toby, and hope to see continued improvement over the coming months.

Yours sincerely, Mr Edward Chandler, Head Teacher.'

Yvonne burst into tears.

'What did I do?' wailed Toby.

24

'I've got an interview,' said Jake to Claire over the phone. 'Assistant in a sports shop. Sounds great. But it means you'll have to bring Toby home on your own if that's OK.'

'OK, I'll do it, though I don't like walking through your estate much when you're not with me. Last time I did I was glared at by a creepy woman in a maroon overall standing at her window, and a scratty old bloke propositioned me like I'm a prostitute.'

There was a stunned silence on the phone, then, 'Eh?' Claire recounted the horrible experiences when she'd walked to his house in the summer. He laughed. 'That sounds like Nutty Norma. She's harmless. And the old geezer was Sid. He's a bit daft and always starts his conversations like that. 'How about it, then?' He thinks he's being profound. You're not telling me you're afraid to walk though our estate? It's not a bad place to live, honestly.' His tone was rather miffed, with an undercurrent of unease.

'And the gear I was offered?'

'Ah. Yeah, well . . . Anyway, I'm so chuffed about this interview. Come and see me off and wish me luck.'

Jake looked so fantastic in his suit, Claire was sure they'd give him the job there and then. She wished him luck with a deep, warming kiss.

★ ★ ★

When Claire met up with Toby after school, she asked, 'Do you want to go straight home, or to the allotments?'

'Allotments of course. I made another bat box and I want to put it up on one of the trees.' He showed her his latest bat box in a strong carrier bag.

'You really love making these bird and bat boxes, don't you?'

'Yeah, it's fun. Bats are cool.'

Claire was round at Jake's a few days later when the post arrived: a thin white envelope bearing regrets. Jake looked so crestfallen she wanted to kiss him better. He went outside into the garden for a minute and she saw him heaving in a few gulps of air before he came back inside. 'I feel all stirred up,' he said. 'Let's go to the Enchanted Garden. I need to chill with a bit of work or I'll go nuts.'

'Me too.'

When they reached the allotments Ted was there working on his plot. He saw them and came over. 'Any news on the job?'

Jake shrugged. 'Didn't get it.'

Ted was still frowning. 'Bad luck. Better luck next time. Anyway, there's something funny going on here. I've just seen some men in suits prowling round the place, snooping. School End, mainly, but they wandered up here past your allotment, right to the end. They

215

didn't look like allotmenteers. More like entrepreneurs. I'm wondering if the town council are thinking of developing the land or selling the whole lot off.'

'Can they do that?' asked Claire.

'I don't think they rightly can, Claire. I don't know the rules offhand. But it occurred to me that now the junior school is closed, that's removed the access problem that made this site unattractive to developers. If they wanted they could build a road in here through the old school grounds and build lots of houses.'

Claire felt a lump rising in her throat. The Enchanted Garden was just a dream after all. Jake would get all funny about not being able to offer her a secure future again, break off their relationship again, and their beautiful allotment and the wildlife-friendly wild-flower meadows would vanish under tarmac and concrete. She would be back to square one, and with a broken heart to boot.

'That's the first time I've seen you do

that in months,' Jake said to her with a frown.

'Do what?'

'Touch your scars like that.'

'Eh?'

'You often used to put your hand up to your scars, especially if you were upset, but you stopped doing it. I bet it's an unconscious thing; you don't know you're doing it.'

Claire raised her hand to her face. She hadn't thought about her scars for a long, long time.

* * *

Claire's little propagator was doing well, and her windowsill was cluttered with cuttings to over-winter. She decided what they really needed for next year was a greenhouse on the allotment. Or even a polytunnel, perhaps. She looked them up on the internet, and found they were quite expensive. She talked about the problem at work, and her boss Janice said that a small polycarbonate greenhouse might do her better as it would cost less to heat, but shouldn't Claire check if they were allowed to have things like that on the allotment before she spent her money? Claire asked Jake. Janice was right; they would have to seek permission.

Jake and Claire decided to go and ask the town clerk, Mrs Patel, in person. They walked slowly into town, hand-in-hand. The town clerk smiled when they went in, but the smile faded when they told her what they wanted to do.

'I wouldn't do that,' she said. 'No. I'm afraid I'll have to decline permission for that. In fact . . . No, sorry Jake, sorry Claire.'

That was when they knew for sure that something was up.

25

The problem with working in the garden centre at the weekend was that most of the other allotment holders worked their plots then, not during the week, so Claire rarely saw them to talk to. Jake asked them if they knew anything. They, too, had seen the men-in-suits, as Claire and Jake started to call them, but nobody knew what was going on.

Tuesday morning Claire's phone went. 'You got the post yet?' Jake asked. 'We were right. There's trouble about the allotments.'

Claire's heart flipped and it had nothing to do with the sexy growl in Jakes voice. 'What sort of trouble?'

'Don't know. We got a letter this morning about a meeting 'to discuss the future of Victoria Road Allotments'. Mum says they've been trying to build on there for years, but never could because it's landlocked. But now that the school has closed she reckons the council want to sell it to a developer, just like Ted suspected.'

Claire said a very rude word, followed by a string of others. 'They can't do that.' She imagined their garden built over with houses crammed in cheek-by-jowl.

'We'll fight it, love. Mum says there are laws protecting allotments. Do you know Ted's phone number? Mum doesn't have it.'

Claire didn't. It was as if none of them existed to each other in the real world. 'I don't even know his surname. Weird that, isn't it?'

Jake said he'd be around shortly. Meanwhile, Claire went online to find out what she could. She found a site by the National Society of Allotment and Leisure Gardeners, and it made very interesting reading indeed. They could fight this, and win. Or so she thought.

* * *

The meeting was in the Town Hall. Fifty chairs were set out, but only about twenty were taken. Elizabeth had come with Claire to give her moral support. Yvonne, Toby and Jake were there, as were Ted and most of the School-Enders. Out at the front of the meeting were the mayor, the clerk, a woman Claire didn't know, and a couple of other men. Ted nudged her. 'Them's the ones who were prowling round the allotments like lost townies.'

The mayor introduced the woman first, as the amenities and leisure manager for the council, Mrs Swann. The mayor then added, 'You all know the clerk, Mrs Patel, of course, but let me introduce you to Mr Terry Mumford and Mr Adrian Falbrook of Perodram Developments.'

Mrs Swann told the meeting that rentals of the Victoria Road Allotments plots had been dwindling for years. Now only twelve of the plots were taken, that the income was only £600 per annum, some of which was being spent on water usage. People just weren't interested in allotments nowadays. Then the Perodram blokes gave a PowerPoint presentation. They wanted to buy the school and the allotment land and build affordable homes and a supermarket on the site, which would benefit everyone (apparently) and bring in lots of jobs (apparently). But to compensate the allotmenteers for their loss, Perodram Developments had bought some land out of town, and would build each of them a shed, build a car park and even a communal clubhouse; lay on water — the works. They showed pictures of something similar they had done in another town. It would be superb. Did anyone have any questions?

Claire raised a hand, feeling her heart thumping. Her other hand was firmly clutching Jake's. He gave it an encouraging squeeze as she said, 'But that proposed site is two miles away, and we don't have a car.'

'And it takes years to get an allotment into good heart, and there are the fruit bushes and other permanent crops on ours,' said Jake. 'We have apple trees that my grandad planted, and they're good croppers. And they're my grandad's. We can't move them; they're too big. Every time I see them or eat an apple off them I think of him.'

'Yes, and there's my asparagus bed,' said a School-Ender, Geoff.

'I have chickens on mine and can pop out to shut them up at night or check on them. It's not exactly ecologically sound to have to jump in the car to go up a few times a day,' said another School-Ender, Danielle. She looked feisty, with punk hair and a nose piecing. She was dandling her darling baby, who gurgled as rumbles of agreement echoed round the room.

'Well, I'm sorry,' said the mayor, 'But let's face it, the Victoria Road Allotments are an eyesore, no allotments have been let recently, and the weeds are head-high in places, which encourages dumping. People who are thinking of renting an allotment take one look and go elsewhere. We made suggestions a few years ago that you form an allotment association and smarten the place up, but that was met with apathy. Time for a new beginning on a new site. I'll take it as a done deal.'

'No you won't,' said Geoff. 'We're not moving. We formed an allotment association two days ago, when young Claire left letters for us on our allotments. We've been looking into this and you have to get permission from the secretary of state for communities and local government before you close allotments.'

'Ah, but since the site is designated a temporary site, not a statutory one, I'm afraid we don't. We've offered you a perfectly good alternative site,' said Mrs Swann. She looked uncomfortable as she shuffled her papers around on the table.

That shook Claire. They had no legal

protection after all. All that work, all that reading up on the internet, and she'd made a mistake. 'But it's not perfectly good,' she said. 'It's too far away, and it won't have the same . . . magic.' Claire could hear the tremor in her voice.

'Magic?' scoffed Mr Mumford, the development man.

'Yes, magic,' said Claire getting to her feet. She told them about living in her mum's flat with no garden, how she and Jake had poured love into the allotment, and how it had saved her from becoming a recluse, restoring her self-confidence; because after her accident she'd been becoming more and more introverted and alone, until she met Jake and worked on his allotment, being creative with him. Elizabeth stood up and clapped, so everyone stood and joined in.

Toby told everyone how he used to help his grandad on the allotment when he was a little boy, then how he had gone off the rails, fallen in with the wrong crowd, and how he felt close to his grandad when he gardened. He also told everyone that he was still having problems — boy, did he blush at that point — and that if they lost their allotment he was worried that he would revert to his bad ways. He looked very young and vulnerable.

Yvonne clapped enthusiastically and stood up. 'It's true. He's a right little tearaway at times, and the only time he's been calm and controllable is when he's digging his allotment. He loves Ted like a grandad and will listen to him when he won't take notice of me.'

'I'm proud of what we've done. Please don't take that away from us,' said Toby.

Others joined in, adding their thoughts and objections.

Mr Falbrook hadn't said anything until that point. Now he stood up. 'It's all very well, but there are only a few of you here. And you, miss . . . ' He nodded at Claire. 'You seem to have treated the place as your own private playground, planting up other allotments with wild flowers, building dens like a kid, putting up bat boxes and bird boxes when you have no right to do so. And now you're asking us to respect that as some sort of lever to prevent development. Humph. There's a desperate need for housing in the southeast, especially affordable homes, which these will be: cluster-homes and flats, built to high specification, but affordable, with a small supermarket on the doorstep to serve the community. It makes sense, and I don't see why these plans, which will benefit lots of people, should be overturned by a handful of latter-day Luddites. And what about your future, miss? Where will you live when you want to leave home? Do you propose to put a tent on your allotment?' he sneered.

When Claire heard that, she regretted mentioning she was living with her mum. He had a cheek — latter-day Luddites indeed. She glared at him. 'Cluster-homes with poxy little gardens;

flats with nothing at all but a few tough shrubs in a sterile communal area. Don't you think that people will need allotments even more if you build these homes? Why do you need to build a supermarket too . . . Why can't you just build on the school site and leave our allotments alone?'

'Yes,' said Jake. 'People need green space like never before. And people want to grow their own food and don't have the space nowadays.'

'They can go to the park for their fresh air, and food is cheap in the supermarkets,' said Mumford. 'And we've offered an excellent alternative. People need affordable homes. Houses with big gardens are just too expensive.'

'Build your sodding supermarket there, out of town,' said Toby, a little wildly. 'Not on our bloody allotments.'

'Don't be so rude, Toby,' said Yvonne half-heartedly.

'Supermarket food is expensive in air miles,' yelled Danielle. Her baby started to howl, everyone started talking at once, and there was uproar. Someone on the front row was scribbling furiously in a notebook.

In the end, the mayor said, 'We hear what you're saying, and will take this back to the next council meeting, but I'm afraid that unless more people show an interest in renting an allotment, we will go ahead and sell the land.'

26

A couple of days later Claire got a phone call from the amenities manager, Mrs Swann. 'We've decided to advertise the allotments. If not enough people take up allotments in the next month, well, I'm sorry Claire, truly sorry, but you'll have to be moved to the new site and Victoria Road Allotments will be sold along with the old school. It's very valuable building land. If I were you I'd get your new association to smarten the place up a bit so it looks less daunting to prospective allotmenteers, and do some advertising of your own. But I didn't tell you that.'

Claire bought the local paper because there was an account of the allotment meeting. 'Uproar at Allotment Meeting', it said. There was also a small advert for the allotments. 'That's not very visible,' said Elizabeth when she looked at it. 'Looks to me like a lip-service advert to show they've tried. If I were you I'd put notes through people's doors, starting with the flats. People on the Arrandel Estate have big gardens so probably aren't interested, but the newer housing estates have tiny gardens. And growing your own is an up-and-coming fad for trendy types.'

That sounded like good advice, which Claire repeated to the burgeoning allotment society. They made sure the paths were mown; they cut back the scrub; they even weed-killed a couple of the plots at School End, and Ted rotavated them. Toby pulled up weeds and tidied up every day after school.

Whilst working on the site, every so often Claire would stop and look into the middle distance, chewing her lip. She loved the allotment — would have been devastated if they'd lost it — but the remarks about affordable housing had hit home, especially if she and Jake decided to get married. She'd looked at house prices and they were horrendous, even on the Arrandel Estate.

* * *

A week before the deadline to let more allotments, Mrs Swann visited the allotments to inspect unofficially. 'My dad had one of these,' she confided to Claire. 'I have a soft spot for the place, but it's becoming derelict. The council are strapped for cash, and it's a handsome offer from the development company.'

They started at School-End, where most of the allotments were taken. Those were well-kept and neat, and some had over-wintering crops on them. They walked through the overgrown bits, which still looked overgrown despite the work, finishing up at Claire and Jake's allotment, sitting on the bench, looking at the wild-life pond. They didn't go as far as the natural pond. There seemed no point. Claire wished it had been summer with the wildflowers busy with butterflies and bees and honeyed scents in the air. But now, in early winter, the place looked neglected and forlorn.

'It's not enough,' said Mrs Swann unhappily. 'I've had no new applications, despite the adverts.'

'You know why that is? I got so desperate I started knocking on doors trying to talk people into having an allotment, and while people fancy having an allotment, they're not committing fifty quid and loads of time and effort on allotments which are about to be sold off. People read about the meeting in the newspaper. So despite the advert, they've been put off the idea of renting one here. At least until all this is settled.' Claire didn't tell her what some had said; that they'd rather have a nice new allotment with a shed on the outskirts of town than one constantly under threat of development. 'It's not fair,' she continued. 'We've worked so hard on this, on a real shoestring, and now it's going to be covered in tarmac and made into a supermarket car park. The new site is too far to walk to easily. Not every day.'

'Can't you learn to drive?'

'I can't really afford to. Nor can I afford a car or the insurance. And anyhow, it won't be the same. And what will the wildlife do? There are newts in my pond. Great Crested Newts, and they're rare. And bats in Toby's bat boxes on that oak tree. That supermarket won't find them a new home, will it? I bet the residents of the new-build homes would shriek at the thought of bats in the loft.'

Mrs Swann looked startled, and stood as if a wasp had stung her. 'I've had an idea. I'll be back later . . . with some people I know.'

27

Claire was nervous and sought Jake's hand as they mounted the steps into the district council offices. 'We're here for the Victoria Road Allotments planning meeting,' said Jake to the woman on the front desk. They filled in visitors' badges and signed the book whilst waiting for their escort. They were shown to the meeting room and invited to help themselves to coffee. Claire gazed round the room. It was plain and workmanlike, with some photographs of previous mayors doing good things for the town. There were world-weary tables pushed together to make one large desk area.

A couple of the School-Enders were already there and smiled as Claire sat down. One was Geoff, who lived in one of the big houses already abutting the allotments. He had a gate directly out onto his allotment. *Lucky thing,* thought Claire. Danielle was there — the young mum with a pierced nose and punky hair who was heavily into organics and owned the chickens — with her baby asleep in its pushchair beside her. These two had been elected treasurer (though they had no funds) and secretary of the fledgling Allotment Association. Claire had been elected chairman, which, she supposed, served her right for starting the idea in the first place. It thrust her into the limelight rather, which she wasn't so happy about, but a year or so ago that would have been utterly unthinkable. Jake was vice-chairman (which made Claire giggle). He helped Claire to some coffee and sat down next to the School-Enders. Mr Romer the parks manager nodded to them. Claire wondered how he would have felt if he'd heard the miffed remarks from Mr Falbrook about planting up the other allotments, since some of the plants they'd used had been given by him. Perhaps he would have felt embarrassed since she had the sneaking suspicion it wasn't strictly allowed.

Mr Mumford from the development company was fiddling with a pen and constantly tugging at his collar. Claire was glad to see that his sneering sidekick Falbrook wasn't with him. The town clerk was there to take the minutes. Mrs Swann was to chair the meeting. There were a couple of people from the local wildlife group whom Claire had met when Mrs Swann brought them over to the allotments to check out the Great Crested Newt sightings, and a couple of other people Claire didn't recognise. Mrs Swann introduced them as being council officers from the planning and housing departments.

After the introductions, Mrs Swann continued, 'I've called this meeting to discuss ways forward with the Victoria Road Junior School site and the allotment site now that Great Crested Newts have been found in the pond at the far end of the allotments. What we want to do is discuss what can be done to mitigate the effects of any building work before planning consent is given, to make sure that we serve the needs of the community with regard to afford-able housing, yet protecting the Great Crested Newts as required by law. I'll open the meeting by asking Sue Harper, who is licensed to handle Great Crested Newts, to discuss what she and Jane Renshaw, also of the Wildlife Group, found when they did their preliminary survey.'

When Claire had met Sue Harper and Jane Renshaw during their survey of the allotments to see if she was right about the rare newts, Sue had been full of praise for the log piles and wildflower meadows. Claire was smug that these tiny creatures would save their allotments for them.

Sue stood up to point to slides on a presentation. 'We have indeed found evidence of Great Crested Newts breeding in the pond at the far end of

Victoria Road Allotments, and a couple in Claire's log piles. This means that all development of that site will have to be postponed and a mitigation plan developed. I'm sure it would help if I briefly described the lifecycle of Great Crested Newts. They breed in water in the spring, then spend most of the year on land, hibernating in the winter in log piles or compost heaps or other such frost-free places. They can wander up to about 500 metres away from the breeding pond and, if you look at your maps in front of you, that almost takes us up to the School-End side of the allotments.' She pointed to the map projected onto the screen.

'So are you saying we can't build at all on the allotments and school site?' asked Mr Mumford. He looked stricken.

'Nothing can be done on the site until the mitigation plan is agreed,' answered Sue.

Mrs Swann said, 'It might be best to avoid any future development of the actual allotment site, but the school site may be able to be developed once a mitigation plan has been devised. That's what we're here to discuss. I have some proposals for the meeting.'

A horrible thought gripped Claire. She'd been viewing the Great Crested Newts as saviours of their enchanted garden, but supposing they were a double-edged sword? 'Pardon me, Sue — when you say that nothing can be done on site, does that mean we can't dig our allotments, and can't garden as we have been doing?'

'I'm afraid not. Now we know there are newts on site we have to take measures to protect them, though I must say the way you have been gardening is very newt-friendly.'

Jake pulled in a breath, and Geoff and Danielle looked horrified. Swirls of despair washed over Claire. They couldn't win; in saving the allotment site she had destroyed their ability to garden there.

Sue gave her a sympathetic glance.

'And the other thing to bear in mind is that the natural pond needs positive management. Ideally it should be about a metre deep, with both vegetation for the eggs, and weed-free parts — the males do a complex mating dance in the water and need space for this, and the females lay eggs individually on vegetation. The pond shouldn't be overshadowed with trees, so those willows need keeping in check. Nor should it be polluted with runoff, and neither should it have any fish in it or many waterfowl using it. It should be surrounded by long grass and vegetation, log piles and rocks, and such territory should be managed without pesticides to ensure the newts have food. A mitigation strategy is more than just not working the site. We have to ensure it's positively managed in favour of the newts.'

Jake sought Claire's hand under the table and squeezed. She glanced at him. He looked worried, really worried.

Mr Romer was looking at the plan. 'If

these newts roam up to 500 metres away I'm surprised I've never seen any in the park. Will we have to start making positive changes in the park as part of this mitigation plan? I'm gradually switching to more permanent planting with things like log piles — would that help?'

Sue nodded. 'We really need to include everything we can in a mitigation strategy. Improving the habitat in the park sounds sensible.'

'I've been talking this over with Sue,' said Mrs Swann. 'What I suggest is that we convert the allotment site to a nature reserve.' Claire heard a distressed groan from Geoff, and Jake tensed. Mrs Swann glanced at Geoff before continuing: 'Part of this reserve will be a buffer zone of allotments between the newt territory and school site, which could still be used for affordable housing.'

'So the School-Enders could keep their allotments?' asked Danielle, a look of hope kindling in her eyes.

'I think that would be a good idea. No supermarket, though. The newts would be kept within the reserve and off the allotments with something called one-way newt fencing, which is angled to allow those which are migrating back to the pond to get to it, but then keeps the newts within the nature reserve.' Mrs Swann looked at Sue.

Sue nodded. 'It takes between two to four years for a newt to reach maturity, during which they are largely terrestrial, so there will be some juveniles scattered all over the site.'

'That way we can go ahead with modified building plans, save the School-End allotments, and protect the newts,' continued Mrs Swann. 'It's the best compromise I can think of.'

'But what about Ted's allotment?' asked Claire. Ted would be furious if he couldn't rotavate his allotment. 'And what about ours?' Claire could feel the tears pricking. Every time they overcame an obstacle, another one appeared. She and Jake exchanged glances.

'I suggest that newt fencing is put round Ted's plot,' said Mrs Swann. 'And pit traps to monitor how many newts there are on his plot . . . I'm sure Sue would advise about this. As for your and Jake's allotment, Claire . . . I think the way it is at the moment is of positive benefit to the site for the newts . . . '

'Yes,' said Sue. 'Use no-dig methods, perhaps. Or better still, why don't you rent a School-End allotment for vegetables and maintain the one you have at present with wildlife and newt-friendly plantings?'

'We can't afford to rent two allotments,' Jake objected. 'I'm out of work and Claire's only got a part-time job.'

'Well, if your allotment is part of the nature reserve, I think something could be managed in that respect,' said Mrs Swann. 'I don't see why you should have to pay for an allotment you can't really use.'

By the time the meeting was over, Mr Mumford had agreed to submit a modified planning application to build on the school site, and had agreed in principle to fund the newt fencing, swallowing a bit over the cost. Mrs Swann had said she would take the proposal to create a nature reserve to the next council meeting (apparently there were funds and grants available for that sort of thing). The Allotment Association (Geoff, Danielle, Jake and Claire) had agreed to consider changing their name to The Friends of Victoria Road Allotments and Nature Reserve and, with guidance from Sue and her Wildlife Group, help with the positive management of the newt site. Jake and Claire were given one of the allotments that Ted and Toby had cleared by the School End to grow their vegetables on. Then the meeting broke up. As they left, Claire saw Mrs Swann and Mr Romer deep in animated conversation.

Claire and Jake were just signing out

at the front desk when Mrs Swann caught up with them. 'Have you got a few minutes, please, you two? Mr Romer and I would like a chat.' They followed her back to the room. 'Let's have another coffee; I'm gasping,' suggested Mrs Swann. 'Don't look so scared, Claire; it's nothing nasty. On the contrary . . . '

'It's like this,' said Mr Romer. 'I've been snooping around your allotment for a while now, and I'm really impressed with what I've seen. You two and young Toby seem to have a natural affinity with wildlife gardening. You mentioned earlier that you're not in work, is that right?'

'I work part-time at a garden centre,' said Claire.

Jake shook his head. 'I haven't got a job.' He suddenly looked bleak.

'Right. No promises, Jake, but I have a groundsman leaving at the end of the month and I have funding for a position as a parks gardener with day-release to the local college for courses in chainsaw safety and so on. I'll want someone sympathetic to wildlife and with good basic gardening knowledge. You'd have to compete with any other candidates, of course — I can guarantee nothing, and the pay is poor and the hours long, but can I hope to see your CV and this application form on my desk as soon as possible?'

Jake's face lit up as he took the forms. 'You can, Mr Romer. You most certainly can.'

Mrs Swann said, 'The other thing is that if we do make the allotments into a nature reserve, we'll need a warden, which there would be funding for . . . part-time, though. I'm just tipping you the wink here, Claire, so you have time to do plenty of reading up. Maybe join that wildlife group as a member . . . I'm sure Sue would help there. No promises, of course . . . '

28

Claire, with the help of the CV brochure she'd found in the charity shop in Erranby, helped Jake rewrite his CV to emphasise his gardening skills. They printed it out, filled in the forms, and he took his application to the council offices before they shut that day. Two days later he had a phone call inviting him for an interview the following week. They both spent ages swotting up about gardening and wildlife. They staged a mock interview with Toby, Yvonne and Claire as the interviewers going through Jake's CV and application form, making him justify all he'd said.

* * *

The allotmenteers held a meeting in Yvonne's garden and agreed to the change in title and role. Claire was grateful to have someone like Geoff to help, because they had to draft a constitution. Toby got very excited about the nature reserve. 'I'll make bat boxes and bird boxes and I'll help build log piles for the newts. I like them. They're like baby dragons,' he said. 'I finish school soon and I'm not doing A-levels.'

'You'll be looking for a job, though,' objected Yvonne. 'I want you kept out of mischief.'

'Yeah, yeah, whatever. In my spare time then.'

* * *

'How do I look?' asked Jake for the tenth time.

'You look amazing,' Claire told him. 'Actually you look drop-dead gorgeous.' He was wearing his new suit, just like he had for the sports shop interview, and he looked mature and respectable as well as gorgeous. Perhaps his poise was due to his athleticism. Whatever, it made Claire feel full of love and pride. She gave him a kiss on the cheek. 'Don't worry. You've done all you can in the way of preparation.'

He pulled her into his arms. 'I'm so nervous, love. It's like our whole future hangs in the balance.'

Claire was allowed to sit in the foyer of the council offices while Jake had his interview. She'd taken a magazine, but she couldn't read it; thoughts jumbled up in her head like a pick-and-mix. Jake sat beside her, studying his thumbs. They were rough from the gardening, indelibly stained in the creases. A delicious memory of those thumbs rasping gently over her nipples caught Claire by surprise.

As they were sitting there, the candidate before Jake came out of his interview. He looked like a nice bloke, and smiled at them as he was leaving. Five minutes later Mr Romer stuck his head round the door with a welcoming smile. 'Mr Handicross, would you like to come in, please.'

'Good luck,' whispered Claire as Jake stood.

Twenty minutes or so slid by, with Claire still flicking blindly through the magazine as if it were some sort of rosary.

A friendly-looking girl came in and told the receptionist she was here for an interview. She sat down opposite Claire to wait. 'You here for the groundsman's job?' she asked.

'No, I'm waiting for my boyfriend.'

'Oh. I hope I get this job. I've done courses, got great marks, and I know what I'm doing. Is your boyfriend qualified?'

'Oh. Which courses have you done?' asked Claire, hoping to deflect the girl away from questions about Jake's qualifications in case he got the job and she didn't and kicked up a fuss.

She went on and on about how good she was. Claire grinned at her, teeth bared, wondering how such a nice-looking person could be so tediously self-centred and arrogant. *I'd hate to work with her*, she thought, *but maybe Mr Romer will have to give her the job. She might claim sex discrimination if he doesn't.* The thought sat like oil in her stomach.

Jake appeared, accompanied by Mrs Swann, who shook his hand and said he should hear one way or another by Friday. Jake looked shattered and any hopes they'd had that getting this job would be an easy ride evaporated like mist. Mrs Swann immediately invited the girl in. Claire took this as a bad sign because there had been a five-minute gap between the man before Jake and Jake's interview. It looked as if Jake had been interviewed just for the sake of it, then, to demonstrate the council were interviewing a diverse group of candidates. Claire couldn't really imagine Mr Romer behaving in such a shabby way, especially having raised their hopes by suggesting Jake apply in the first place. Maybe they had better candidates and his hands were tied.

Outside the council offices Claire gave Jake a long hug. 'Well done.' She didn't tell him about the girl's splendid qualifications.

'I think I've blown it, love. It was awful. Gruelling. Let's go home, I'll get changed, and we can go to the allotments for an hour or two. Give Ted a hand with his newt fencing, perhaps.'

*   *   *

Ted grumbled the whole time he was installing his newt fencing, even though the cost of his materials had been funded by the development company. When it was finished he grudgingly said, 'Hmn, it's not bad really . . . and it'll keep the carrot fly off me carrots with any luck.'

*   *   *

Friday arrived. Claire went over to Jake's house early and they waited anxiously for the post. Yvonne was there because she had the morning off as she was on duty for late surgery. The phone rang. Jake's hands trembled as he answered it. 'Speaking . . . ' Yvonne looked tense. Jake's face split into a huge grin. 'Thanks. That's brilliant news. Look forward to it. Bye.' He put the phone down. 'I've got it. I've got the job. They've put the contract in the post.' He danced round the kitchen like a Masai warrior. 'Marry me, Claire. Will you marry me?'

'What kind of way is that to propose to your lady?' scolded Yvonne. 'Do it properly, silly boy.'

Jake sobered up and got down on one knee. 'Claire, my darling Claire. I love you and I want to spend the rest of my life with you. Will you marry me?'

29

'Stop, woman!' commanded Jake in his sexy rumble. Claire froze, key halfway into the lock on the door of their new home in Scholars Mews on the old school site. 'Now we're married I want to do this properly.' He opened the door, lifted her up and carried her across the threshold, then gave her a toe-tingling kiss. 'Ours, our home.'

Claire melted into his embrace. 'We're so lucky, aren't we? Being low-paid council workers has its advantages. I'm glad we qualified for affordable housing.'

'Um . . . and I can walk to work, while you can look out of the bedroom window onto your place of work — well, one of your places of work.'

'We've left the suitcase outside,' Claire squealed. They were just back from honeymoon: just a long weekend in Florence, all they could afford, but all they needed.

Jake went out and lifted it in. 'Better get this lot washed and dried. We don't want to have it hanging around on Friday if we're having a house-warming party.' He opened the suitcase, and they divided the washing up into piles and put a load on.

'I want to have a look round the reserve,' said Claire.

'I want to try our new bed out,' said Jake.

Claire thought that was a much better idea.

★　★　★

Friday. The food was ready, the drinks were ready, Jake looked like a hero, and Claire's heart was thumping. The doorbell — their doorbell — made her jump even though she was waiting for it. Ted was on the doorstep bearing a couple of bottles of elderflower wine. 'Ted, come in; you're the first. That

means I have time to show you round.'
Her mum and Yvonne knew what the house looked like, but Ted hadn't seen it. The door opened straight into the kitchen diner-cum-living room, with a downstairs loo and utility room under the stairs. They had a second-hand pine dining table and chairs, and a new two-seater sofa, with a couple of beanbags as extra furniture. The washing machine was a wedding present from Elizabeth, while Yvonne had bought them the sofa and bed. Toby, who now had a job at the supermarket collecting trolleys, had given them some bed linen: paid for, most definitely not nicked.

Claire showed Ted upstairs to the first floor, which had their bedroom and bathroom. Ted went to the window. 'Good view,' he commented. 'Just right for the nature reserve warden to look out on her kingdom.' He cast Claire an amused look. 'I can see young Toby's nature trail very well from here.'

'It's not his, really. He just helped

build it. Mind you, I reckon being a volunteer on the nature reserve helped get him that supermarket job.' Claire showed Ted up the second flight of stairs to the second bedroom. It had a skylight window and a desk with Claire's computer. 'I didn't realise how much paperwork being a warden involves,' she said. 'I love my jobs, Ted. And Jake loves his. I'm the luckiest girl in the world.'

The doorbell rang, so they went downstairs again. Claire helped Ted to a beer, then went to mingle with their other guests: all the School-Enders, Yvonne, Toby, Elizabeth, Elspeth Swann, Inderjit Patel the clerk, Mr Romer, Sue and Jane from the wildlife group, even Mr Mumford from the development company, who had grown more enthusiastic about the nature reserve as time had gone by. Jake came and wrapped an arm round Claire and they talked to their guests as one entity, Claire-and-Jake.

Ted was sipping his beer when Claire said to him, 'Well Ted, looks like the allotment site was saved by newts after all. Do you still say wildlife belongs in the wild?'

He pondered for a moment, then smiled. 'Too right it belongs in the wild. I have a fence round my plot to keep that pesky wildlife out.'

Claire laughed. 'So you do, Ted. So you do.'

THE END